I0615973

New Attitude

By

Kathryn R. Biel

Kathryn R. Biel

NEW ATTITUDE

Copyright © 2017 by Kathryn R. Biel

ISBN-13: 978-1-949424-26-3

Resilient Books

This book is a work of fiction. Names, characters, places, and incidents are either products of the author's imagination or are used fictitiously and any resemblance to actual persons, living or dead, business establishments, events or locales is purely coincidental.

All rights reserved.

No part of this book may be reproduced, scanned, or distributed in any printed or electronic form or by any electronic or mechanical means including information storage and retrieval systems, without permission in writing from the author. The only exception is by a reviewer, who may quote short excepts in a review. Please do not participate in or encourage piracy of copyrighted materials in violation of the author's rights. Purchase only authorized editions.

Cover design by Becky Monson.

Dedication

To my cousins (yes, all of you), but especially Lauren, Genny, and David for helping me out so I didn't actually have to get up and visit NYC.

Chapter 1

Done.

That's what the note says. One blippin' word. Done. He doesn't even give me the courtesy of a pronoun. Would it have taken that much more effort to say "I'm done?" No, it wouldn't. But for Stan, the lazy turd, perhaps it was just too much.

You know, like being married to me.

Lots of colorful words run through my head right now. And if my five-year-old weren't standing next to me, believe you me, the expletives would be flowing like hot lava right now.

I should have guessed this was why Stan dropped Fleur at my mom's. Silly me. I figured he was working to support our family. I didn't realize he was done with our family. *Done.*

"Mommy, did you change my room too?"

I'm stuck in the kitchen, staring at his incredibly verbosely written note. Amazing how one word can rivet my attention so completely.

Fleur breaks my concentration by tugging on my arm. "Mommy, why did you change the house? I don't like it."

"Huh?" I struggle to focus on her. My mind is spinning and whirling. "What are you talking about? I just walked in. I haven't been home in ..."

Well, crap.

Fleur's pulled me into the living room. Or the space formerly known as the living room. Now it's an empty shell. I cannot believe he did this. Now it makes sense. Obviously, he was so busy emptying out our stuff that he couldn't possibly have found time for more than a one-word explanation. The only thing he left were the pictures on the walls. Except for the large Kandinsky reproduction. Now a large blank space occupies the long wall in the room. Above where the couch used to be. Opposite the void left by the TV. Stan gave it to me for our first anniversary because I loved *Circles in a Circle*. How could he take that?

Oh no, what else did he take? Where did Fleur go?

She's contentedly playing in her room, happy to be home. Relief fills my body, making me go slack against the doorway of Fleur's intact bedroom. Oh thank goodness. I don't think I could have taken it if he took her stuff. Speaking of stuff ...

You have got to be kidding me.

Our—my—bedroom looks like a tornado went through. A tangled pile of blankets on the floor. A deserted pillow. An overturned lamp. My clothes, in a heap. Gone is the bed. The nightstands. The dresser. The TV. Why does he need both TVs? He always hated the bedroom TV—said it was too small. Yeah, if only I'd complained about things that were too small ...

Who does this?

Why? Why would Stan do this to me? Sure we fought over stupid, married couple stuff. Nothing major though. Frankly, I always thought I was lucky because Stan was easy going. He was the most laid-back Prince Charming ever.

Until the contest, that is.

I wish I could say my partner was the super-supportive type, but that'd be a lie. He wasn't exactly *unsupportive* either. He simply, well, he didn't care. But it was a purposeful not caring. A passive aggressive non-acknowledgment. You know, it's not every day that you audition and make it through three rounds of cuts to make it onto a reality TV design show. Heck, I didn't even think I'd make it.

Maybe I saw Stan's jaw set a little when I told him I made the show and would be gone for at least eight weeks. But it's not like he objected, or said anything at all. And it was about time I got to go away. With him on the road all the time, I'd certainly done my time as a single parent over the past five years with Fleur. Not that I mind, because my baby girl is my whole world. I didn't think he'd mind, really. Apparently I was wrong. And here I was, so impressed at how he'd stepped up into the primary caregiver role for Fleur.

Fleur. Oh my God, how could he do this to her? Is he going to want to see her? Am I even going to let that happen? How can I? How can I not?

Well, let's face it— he left me, not her. Not yet, at least.

He'd better not have left her. On the other hand, I sort of want to inflict bodily harm on him, so it might be better if I don't have to see him all the time.

"Mommy, where are you going to sleep?" Fleur's tugging on my shirt hem. I'm so focused on the bazillion thoughts racing through my mind, most involving ways to torture Stan, that I didn't even hear her come in. I look down at her, too flummoxed to even put together an answer.

"Mommy, what happened to your bed?"

"I ... um ... I guess Dad must have needed it."

"You can sleep with me if you want." Her voice is so little, so sweet, so innocent. Oh, to see things through the eyes of a five-year-old. I don't know how to tell her there's no way my size fourteen rear end is going to fit in the daybed with her. And her sixty-five hundred stuffed animals. Okay, that may be a slight exaggeration, but the last time I counted there were over thirty in her bed. That doesn't even account for the ones in the toy box. Either way, it doesn't leave much room for me. Not that I'll be sleeping much tonight.

Where could he have gone?

I need to call him and find out what's going on, I mean besides the obvious. "Mommy, what are we going to do about this mess?"

"I don't know, honey. I don't know." I need to sit down, but short of Fleur's bed, there's not much left in the house to sit on. How could he have done this?

"Does Daddy know what happened? Should we call the police and tell them someone took all our stuff? Why didn't they take my stuff? I'm just happy they left my things. Miss Sparkles is very valuable, you know. And my dollhouse. That's the most valuable thing."

Normally, I adore my little girl's bright and inquisitive nature. However, today it puts me over the edge. The tears I'd been holding back spring forth, gushing and wracking my body with sobs.

Fleur rushes me, throwing her tiny body on top of me. "Oh, Mommy, don't cry. Daddy will help find your things. Call him to come home."

The irony of her statement makes me laugh. Not a happy little chuckle but that maniacal laugh that comes with insanity. Sort of fitting at the moment. With the back of my hand I brush the tears from my face and stand up.

"We're going to Grammy's." I try not to notice the disappointment in Fleur's face. I can read her like a book. I know she was looking forward to being in her own room tonight. Me too. I don't know what else to do though. After eight weeks filming *Made for Me*, all I wanted was my own bed. Now I don't even have a bed. Stan. That bastard.

Our bags are still by the front door where I'd dropped them. Once they're loaded back in the car, we head back to my mom's. I don't even know what I'm going to say to her. This is so mortifying. It's bad enough that he left me. Cleaning out my stuff is over the top. Oh gosh, if that's what he did to our things, what did he do to our bank accounts? The pit in my stomach grows to epic proportions, and I sort of want to vomit. Actually, no sort of about it. My grip on the steering wheel tightens in a near futile attempt to maintain control of my vehicle.

Once I pull into my mom's driveway, I send Fleur into the house, while I pull up our banking information on my phone. My only hope is that since Stan is technologically challenged, he won't know how to access our bank accounts. He doesn't use the computer and can barely work his smartphone. A minute amount of relief rushes through my body. A smartphone is only as smart as its user. Stan hasn't touched the bank account. I go in and reset all the security information, this time using information from the TV show, rather than my normal passwords and background questions. That'll show him.

I have no doubt Stan will come for the money next. Let's face it, the majority of it is his anyway. I haven't worked much since Fleur was born. It was too hard to hold down a nine-to-five with him on the road all the time. I know driving a truck is hard work. I appreciate the sixteen-hour days he put in so that I could be home with our daughter. He never seemed to mind the long hauls. It didn't bother him to be gone for three or five days at a time. I used to joke that he could have another family out there, and I'd never know since he was gone all the time.

Son of a—

Ten bucks says I could now be the subject of a *Dateline Mystery* or *20/20* show entitled "His Secret Life."

Don't ask me how I know, but I know. He's got some chippy somewhere. She's probably a size two and doesn't have blue hair. Even though he always said he liked my brightly colored hair, I bet he has a secret fetish for a cookie-baking Betty Crocker of a wife.

To be clear, that's never been me.

Oh gosh, what if he has a bunch of kids too? They'd be Fleur's siblings. I guess that would come in handy if she ever needs an organ or something, but otherwise, I don't want her to have anything to do with those lowlifes who stole our life.

Wait— what if *we're* the ones who stole *their* life? What if they came first, and then we're the scum who took him away? No, that couldn't be. It wouldn't make sense for him to clear out my stuff if we were the new family. Unless, of course, he had a family before us, and now he's setting up with *another* family. Cripes, we're going to end up as the next *Sister Wives* show. Nope, I won't participate. Of course I won't. Because my mind is getting ahead of me. This can't be the reality. I've known Stan too long. We dated for five years before we got married and then were married for five years before we had Fleur. And now she's five. Fifteen years this man has been in my life. No way he has another family, let alone two. That's just too unrealistic, even for my warped mind.

There's got to be a logical explanation.

Chapter 2

"You know, I never liked him." My mom slides a tumbler of something alcoholic into my hand. Well, it'd better be alcoholic. I can't tell yet, because I haven't lifted my head from her kitchen table in about two hours. She's been entertaining Fleur, which has been a godsend. On the other hand, the constant berating of my husband—that I could do without.

"Huh. Didn't seem that way at my birthday. You two sang a pretty karaoke duet, if I remember correctly."

"I, ah, well, I mean, I always thought you could do better."

"Jeez, that's funny because I sort of remember you telling Stan at our wedding that you never thought you'd find anyone to take me, and you couldn't believe how lucky I was to have found such a wonderful man."

"Oh, for Pete's sake Kira, I'm trying to be supportive!"

With a huff, she walks away, and I'm left to continue my wallowing. I haven't heard from Stan, not that I'd expected to anyway. And no way on God's green earth am I calling him. Heck no. It's day two of the wallow. I'd like to keep on this schedule for about, oh, two more months, but I have to fly out to Montabago in three days for the royal wedding. I'll be there, helping Michele with any last-minute details. It was nice of her to invite me. I thought for sure she'd take her new boyfriend, but she asked me to be her date for the festivities. I so don't feel like going. I mean, wasn't it enough that I spent an extra three weeks helping her out to win the finals?

Three days ago, I was excited to be going to a royal wedding. I couldn't wait to get home and see my family for a few days and then be off again for a few more. One last hurrah before life settled back into our old routine.

Ha. As if.

There's no routine. There's no home. There's no husband. No nothing. Just me, my daughter, my nagging mother, and alcohol. Praises be for that. I lift my head enough to down the contents of the glass.

I splutter out the contents. Water? Why would she give me water? I need vodka. Lots of vodka. *All the vodka.* On the other hand, I have been either drunk or hungover since I got to my mom's house. I probably should get myself together and spend some time with Fleur.

I cannot believe Stan did this. Still. It's not getting any easier. Frankly, it's getting worse. I can't imagine things ever getting better. My husband walked out on me. I just lost the biggest career opportunity I've ever had, and the whole world knows because I did it on TV. I weigh more now than I ever did pregnant.

And to top it all off, I have to go be happy to watch people get married.

All I want to say is bah humbug, and it's spring time, not Christmas. Bah humbug.

"Are you done?"

Oh yeah. Mom's back.

"Done with what?"

"Your pity party. You've got stuff to do."

"I'm not doing anything besides getting myself another drink and eating myself into a stupor."

"Can you eat yourself into a stupor?"

Okay, now I think she's doing this just to get on my nerves. "Mom, don't test me. You know what I mean."

"Don't be snippy. I get that you're in a bad mood. You've made that plenty obvious to me and your daughter. Are you going to let that be the rest of your life?"

"It's only been two days, Mom. I'm allowed to be miserable."

"But two days to your child seems like an eternity. She can't watch you be like this day after day." Dang. She's got me. I sit up and take another drink of the water. Maybe it is time to sober up. I have to leave Fleur in a few days again. What if she starts to get a complex about being abandoned? Maybe I shouldn't leave her.

"Mom, do you think I should stay? It's probably not the best idea to leave Fleur right now. I don't want to mess her up permanently."

"No, Kira. You need to go. You worked so hard for this— you need to see it through."

"It's not like they're my designs though."

"No, but Michele picked you to help her. Without you, she wouldn't have won. You know it. I know it. She knows it, which is why she invited you to the wedding. I'll keep Fleur. I would have even if Stan were still in the picture but had to leave for work. Fleur will get to see her beautiful mommy on TV, hopefully, and will know how talented and wonderful she is."

When did my mom get so smart? I'm almost positive she wasn't this smart when I was a teenager. I would have remembered that.

I hope Fleur thinks I'm smart someday. Of course, she'll probably spend most of the next thirty years thinking I'm an idiot because, well, you know what they say about payback.

"Okay, then, well, what do I do first? I don't know even where to start."

My mom chews her lip for a minute. It's her manipulation face. She's processing how to present the information so that she basically is telling me exactly what she wants me to do but in a way so I think it's my idea. She's done it all my life. Sadly, I only figured it out about ten years ago.

"Well, let's see. Where do you think we should start?"

I tell you, this woman is a master manipulator. She should have been in hostage negotiations or at the U.N. or something. She missed her calling.

"Mom, just tell me, okay? Tell me what to do. How do I plan for a trip when my life is in shambles? Where do I begin?" I pause. Oh crap, I set her up. She's going to start singing a Julie Andrews song. I cannot handle *The Sound of Music* right now. I have to nip this in the bud. "And yes, I know I start at the very beginning. Please don't sing."

"What's the deal with the house?"

"He took a large majority of the furniture. You know that."

"What's the status of your lease?"

"Oh, um, I'm not sure."

"Then that's number one. You need to put on a low-cut top and cry some good tears and see if you can convince your landlord to let you break the lease."

Normally I'd say it would be too sad to give up my home, but it's not home anymore. Stan made sure of that. It's a place that I used to call home. Even if I got all new things, I would never feel the same about it. Mom's right. I need to cut ties and start as fresh as possible as soon as possible.

Over the next three hours—oh wait, it only felt that long—Mom outlines a plan for what I need to do in the next few days. She's got her legal pad and extra-fine-point pen, jotting everything down. She's a list maker. I'm not, but if it gives her some perverse pleasure, she can have at it. She's been single for twenty years. She needs something that gets her rocks off.

I'm sort of dozing off when I vaguely hear her say something that doesn't sound quite right. "What was that?" I try to open my eyes a bit wider, hoping it will help me wake up.

"I'll call Melissa and see if I can get you a hair appointment. It's going to take a long time to get it to where it needs to be, but I think she's up for the challenge."

"Um, yeah, no." I cannot believe we're going to have this conversation. Again.

"Kira Marie, it's not like you can go to the wedding of ... whoever those people are, looking like that."

Oh. My. God.

"Mom, I've been dying my hair for how long now?"

Through gritted teeth she spits, "Twenty years."

"And what did I tell you?"

The muscle in her cheek twitches under the tension. "That I would get your wedding and that's it."

"And what color was my hair for my wedding?"

"Brown."

"That's right. I lived up to my end of the deal. End of discussion."

"But your hair—"

"Is gorgeous. I will need it touched up. Should I stay in this color palette? I call it peacock. I saw the next thing I'm going to try. It's actually a silver-gray base with pastel colors running through it. It reminds me of a unicorn. But I don't know that it's formal enough for the wedding. What do you think? Let me see if I can find a picture on Pinterest so you know what I'm talking about."

I know I'm purposefully being obtuse, but so is she. Ever since I first dyed my hair, she's been flipping out. And, like I'd ever go to her hairdresser. I'll call Emay, my girl. When I auditioned for *Made for Me*, my hair was a bright green. But there were times when I felt too much like Kermit the Frog, so I added blues and teals and just a hint of purple to get my current peacock look. I will need to freshen it up before I go to

Europe. That's the tough thing about the color—it doesn't last long. Even with the special, heinously expensive shampoo, it tends to fade.

I keep talking, mostly so my mom can't get a word in edgewise and argue with me. "It will be a little tricky to find a gown that works with my hair. I don't have time to make one. Will you help me?"

There's nothing my mom loves more than shopping. Her eyes light up, and I know I've got her. If only everything else in my life were so easy.

Chapter 3

"Hey."

I don't know how to respond to this. Stan's voice is making me want to cry and rage all at the same time.

"You there?"

"Yeah." I'm going with rage. A controlled rage. Ice-cold rage. I can do this.

"So, I'm filing for divorce."

I can't do this. I pinch my eyes shut, hoping to prevent the tears from bursting forth. Crying in an airport is so not cool.

"Kira?"

"I heard you." My voice is tight.

"I'm filing for divorce."

"I got that. Your note really said it all." I glance at my watch. I've got about twenty minutes before I board.

"Note? Oh, yeah, I was in a hurry."

"Apparently. Was the moving truck leaving without you?"

"What do you care? You left me."

"Left you? I was *working*. You know, like when you're gone five days a week."

"You weren't working. You didn't even get paid."

Well, he's got me there.

"Why are you being so nasty? I don't have time for this right now."

"What are you doing that's so important?"

I'm about to fill him in on my upcoming transatlantic flight. We'd always planned on touring Europe together when Fleur was a little older. At least I'm getting there before he is. "It's not really any of your concern, now is it? Just tell me what you want from me."

"I can't get into the bank account."

A slow, evil grin spreads across my face. "Huh. Imagine that."

"You can't do that. It's illegal."

"I'm pretty sure taking all our joint possessions is illegal too. Especially the things you've gifted to me." I want my damn painting back. Not that I have a wall to hang it on, but that's neither here nor there.

"Yeah, whatever. I don't want to have to use a lawyer."

"I'm pretty sure to get divorced we have to use a lawyer." The announcements crackle over the loudspeaker, forcing me to pause for a minute. When it ceases, I resume. "I won't be around for a little while, but I'll look into it when I get a chance."

"Isn't the show done? What are you doing now? And where are you? Why is it so loud?"

"Stan, you don't get the right to ask me this anymore. We're *done*." I can practically taste the acid in my voice.

"Fine. When do you think you can file the papers?"

"A., It's not that easy. B., Slow your roll. C., What's the rush?" I know what's coming, but I still don't want to hear it.

"I, um, met someone."

Whomp. There it is. Even though I knew it was coming, hearing those words doesn't make it any easier.

"I figured as much." I want to know everything, yet nothing at the same time. "How long?"

There's a pause on the line. Oh no, this is not a good sign.

"A while."

A while? What the heck is that supposed to mean? I ask as much.

"Well, um, about two years."

Suddenly, there is no air. Two years? Two years!

The announcements blast again, mercifully sparing me from totally losing it.

"I have to go. If she's waited two years, she can wait a little longer. Oh, and your daughter is fine, thanks for asking."

I hang up and immediately turn off my phone. I miss the good ole days when you could slam down the receiver instead of angrily tapping a screen to disconnect. Stupid technological advancements.

Two years. Two years. Two years. The words march through my brain like a demented song. Two years ago, Fleur was three. While I was potty training our daughter, Stan was with her. While I held our baby through ear infection after ear infection and then finally surgery to put tubes in her ears, he was with her.

I need a drink. I need all the drinks. I wish I were flying first class so I could get something before take-off. I wonder how many drinks they'll let me have on this flight. The menu stuffed in the seat pocket informs me that beer is complimentary on international flights. Beer it is. I'm good with that.

Three beers later, I'm not feeling so hot. Normally three beers wouldn't have much of an effect on me, but things seem to be spinning that usually don't. In any case, I don't feel that great. It's all sorts of hot in here, and I feel a wave of paranoia about closed spaces wash over me.

I lean my head back against the seat and pray that the old wives' tale about lice not liking dyed hair is true. I add fear of lice to my mental list of things I hate about flying. It's helping me to focus on something other than Stan or the thought of throwing up. Both are competing for my attention and neither is particularly pleasant.

"Dear, you probably shouldn't have drank so much. Your face is as green as your hair." The old dude in the seat next to me finally makes his entrance. He's been staring at me since I boarded and sat down. I know it's the hair. I get it a lot. Usually people of his generation are highly critical regarding my vibrant locks. I've been called all sorts of names, most as colorful as my hair. I know I shouldn't engage, but I can't help myself. Loose lips sink ships.

"I got some bad news right before I boarded. Plus, I hate flying, so the drinking seemed like the only thing to do." I want to add that I was sort of hoping to fall asleep so I wouldn't have to make awkward conversation with total strangers. I haven't had *that* much to drink, thankfully.

I sort of expect him to ask either about my hair or what the bad news was, but my seatmate doesn't. Instead, he surprises me by launching into a history lesson about Jonas Salk and the development of the polio vaccine. Apparently, Edward (he introduced himself about forty-five minutes into his talk) had been on the janitorial staff at the University of Pittsburgh while Salk was working on the vaccine. Edward's younger brother, Leo, had had polio, so Edward was happy to do anything to help end the epidemic, even if it meant sweeping floors.

I'm so engrossed in Edward's tale that I don't notice how quickly time is elapsing, until the captain announces our descent into Charles de Gaulle. I have a connecting flight to Montabago. A quick glance at my watch reveals that we're on time. At least I think we are. I'm stumped trying to figure out the time difference when the captain announces the local time of six a.m. My watch reads midnight. I guess I lost a night's sleep then. My next flight departs at seven-thirty, so I should have plenty of time to get some water and go to the bathroom.

"My dear, is Paris your final destination? You must be in the industry with hair that fashionable."

"No but yes. I'm a fashion designer, but I'm off to Montabago."

"For the wedding?"

"Why, yes, but how ...?"

"My wife loves all the royal watching. She can no longer travel, so I'm taking one last business trip, solo. After this, I'm done."

"Certainly you are of retirement age?" No offense to Edward, but either he's closing in on eighty or he's lived a very hard life.

"Eighty-four should make the cut, I'd think."

"Eighty-four? I never would have thought that. You look fantastic." It's not just his face. As we're deplaning, he moves with a smoothness that I wouldn't expect from a man of his duration on earth. I think of my own grandparents who were always old. Or at least always seemed that way.

"Age is, in large part, a state of mind. Most things are you will find."

We part with a fond farewell and wishes for safe travels. If only I could live as productive of a life as he did. Following his work for Dr. Salk, Edward himself returned to school and went into medical research. He's actually Dr. Edward Something-or-other, but told me he hates the pretense of the title. If he were only fifty years younger and not married, he'd be the perfect man for me.

The thought of another man startles me. Not that I've had a lot of time to process life without Stan, but it's obvious he's not coming back. And I would hate myself if I ever took him back. Even though the idea of returning to how things were would be tempting, there are some things you just can't get over. The fact that he's been unfaithful for two years is one of them. Plus, I'm pretty peeved about how he left Fleur.

That I never saw coming. I mean, true, he was apprehensive about being a father. It's part of why we waited so long before trying. I don't feel like I pushed him into it, but let's just say I was ready a lot sooner than he was. However, from the first moment he held Fleur, I knew he was smitten. I can still see his face in the delivery room, melting into a smile and saying, "I know some babies are really funny looking, but this one's pretty cute."

He was right, of course. Right from the beginning, Fleur was adorable. Even more adorable than Fleur was her relationship with Stan. I never would have pictured his big, burly tattooed body dressed up in a floppy, purple lace hat and drinking imaginary tea. I want to smile at the memory, but now the tears escape my tenuous hold on them. How could he do this to me? How could he do this to her? Doesn't he know that kids from broken homes are usually messed up, especially the girls?

I hastily head into the nearest bathroom. I draw on my high school French to remember that femmes means women. Thankfully I remember enough to navigate the airport without too much difficulty. In *les toilettes*, doing what you do in there, from outside my stall, I hear the voices of two women rapidly speaking French, and it hits me. I'm in France. It may only be the airport, but it's France.

My whole life, I've dreamed of this. Paris. Stan always promised me we'd go. In hindsight, I don't think he ever had any intention of taking me. He'd tell me that because he was on the road all the time; when he was off, he didn't want to travel. Certainly that made sense to me at the time.

Now I wonder though. I feel like my whole life has been a lie. It probably has been.

Chapter 4

Jet lag blows. I don't know what day it is. I don't know what time it is. I'm not sure if I'm hungry or dehydrated or what. Thank goodness I arrived with a few days to sort myself out before the wedding. And there's still work to be done. It's Michele's responsibility, of course, but it's not like I'm going to sit back and watch her work. I made the dresses right alongside her. Yes, these are her designs, but it's just as much my labor in the craftsmanship. It was three weeks at breakneck pace to make the attire for the entire wedding party—groomsmen, bridesmaids, flower girl and ring bearer, groom, and the bride, which was the point of the whole contest to begin with.

I never thought I'd get onto the show in the first place. Even making it to the third round was beyond what I hoped for. Well, I did want to go all the way, but it became glaringly obvious to me that I wasn't cut out for the competition. I spent most of my down time in my room, trying not to have a nervous breakdown. I missed Fleur so much that it hurt. The other contestants were partying it up most of the time.

Michele and I were roommates, and she navigated a delicate balance between hiding out and hooking up. Not hooking up-hooking up, because she's not that kind of girl, but at least a little flirting and sucking face with a fellow contestant. Not that I blame her. She's young and single. Asher is hot. If only I'd known Stan wasn't honoring our marriage vows, I could have taken a shot. Not really, because why would someone like that look at someone like me? Pasty white skin. Cellulite. Stretch marks. The only thing I like is my hair. I'm too tall. Too pale. Too curvy.

Asher had his pick of the contestants, both male and female. It doesn't surprise me he went for Michele. Petite and blond, the epitome of cute. Not to mention insanely talented. She's got no formal design training, save a semester at my alma mater, Columbus School of Design, but it didn't matter. She won the contest with Asher placing in second. I bet that burned his griddle to play second fiddle.

Last I heard, he'd asked Michele to move to London with him. I never got the story of why she turned him down. The way she mooned over him during the contest, I thought for sure she'd say yes. She's got someone new now. I'll have to get the details the next time we're alone. I wonder if she's one of these girls who moves from one dude to the next, never pausing to be alone with herself.

Like me.

I haven't been alone in fifteen years. But in many ways, I've been alone a lot. With Stan's job, I'd say I was by myself about half the time. Truth be told, sometimes having him home bothered me. Fleur and I had a groove, and sometimes Stan got in our way.

I need to keep thinking this way. About how I'm better off without him. About how I deserve better. Two years!

"Yoo hoo! Are you decent?" Michele floats in. We're in this super-fancy suite in the royal palace. We've got a living room, complete with a fireplace. Two bedrooms flank the common area. Private bathrooms, of course. I sort of expected the faucets to be made of gold, but they were Grohe. I wonder if they have Home Depot here in Montabago. This suite is certainly nicer than anywhere I've ever stayed or could have dreamed of staying.

"Coming."

Michele is anxiously pacing the living room. I'm nervous for her. She's about to go to the last fitting for the bridal party. "Do you want me to come with you? That way I can help with anything that needs to be done."

"Don't you want to go on a tour or something? See the country."

Normally, I'd jump at the chance to have a real European experience. Today, I'm not feeling it. If I went, I think I'd just mope around and not really absorb anything. I'm probably better off keeping my mind and my hands busy. "Nah. There are more important things, like making sure every gown is perfect."

Michele tears up a little. "I'm so nervous I could puke. What if something happens? What if the gown doesn't fit Maryn?"

"Maryn? Are you on a first name basis now?" The duchess and soon-to-be princess always seemed aloof and a bit snobby. I can't imagine calling her by her first name.

Michele smiles sweetly. "Yeah, actually, she's really nice. I know that's not how she seemed on the show, but she is. She's pretty lonely. I guess it's hard being royalty."

I glance around at our digs. "Oh yeah, I can tell how rough things must be." In my mind I'm thinking that I don't even have a place to live. Come to think of it, Michele was in the same boat while we were on the show. She was having financial difficulties, so she'd given up her apartment and was moving back in with her parents. Winning the show took care of that issue, I'm sure.

For the first time, I'm glad I didn't win. I wouldn't want Stan to be able to claim half of my winnings. Nope, I'm not going there. I'm not thinking about him now. I need to focus. I need to sew.

"I'll come with you. After all, we've come this far. I'm not going to leave you hanging at the last minute."

"Are you sure? I can get someone to take you around. It's a beautiful country, and the food is to die for."

"Will they still feed us even if we're working?"

Michele smiles. "Totally. I think I've gained five pounds since I got here. Or maybe it's because I'm so happy."

"Yeah, you seem it. Winning looks good on you." She does look good. So much more relaxed than when we were on the show. The stress during filming, not to mention the sheer fatigue, took its toll on all of us. That's not the only change with Michele though. She's happy. Truly happy. It exudes from every pore.

I envy her.

Even though this is still a stressful time, there's a lightness to her movement. Practically a skip in her step. Meanwhile, I feel so weighed down I can barely lift my foot to take the next step.

And even worse, I can't imagine ever being light again. Not just in weight but mentally.

I'm a thirty-five-year-old, overweight, soon-to-be divorced mom. I'm sure I'll have the men lining up. Not that I even want to think about men right now. Ugh, no thank you. Stan's put me off men for a while. A long while. Ain't no way I'm going back there.

"Kira?"

"Oh, what? Sorry. I didn't hear you."

Michele's brow crinkles. "Yeah, I got that. Are you okay?"

"Yeah, fine. Still getting used to the time change and all. What did you say?"

"I asked if you were ready to go. There'll be coffee and tea downstairs where we're doing the fittings and alterations. They've got a whole room set up for us. It's pretty sweet!"

I can do this. I can focus on something other than my pathetic life.

Chapter 5

I can't stop crying. I thought it was socially acceptable at a wedding, but this is a little ridiculous. Mostly because Michele and I are the only ones crying. We're in a cathedral with about a million people—no joke, at least seven hundred—and we're the only ones even showing tears. I look around at the European royalty and upper crust. Nope, not a drop.

Michele's a mess. Her makeup is starting to run. She deserves this though. Duchess—*Princess*—Maryn looks absolutely fantastic. Fantastic isn't even the right word. Like Grace Kelly but better. Didn't think Grace Kelly could be better? The gown, and overall look, Michele designed for the princess is beyond perfection. I'm so proud of her, and so proud to have been a part of it.

But being at a wedding is making me think of my own wedding day and about my sham of a marriage. The more I think about it, the more upset I get. So it's been two years with *this* one. Who's to say if there were others before her? I never pegged Stan for a cheater. I guess I didn't know him at all. The tears pick up again.

Michele leans over and whispers, "I know, right? She looks beautiful."

I should let my friend have this moment, but before I know it, the truth rushes out. "Stan left me."

Oh crap. I didn't mean to say that now.

"What?"

"When I got home after the final taping, he was gone. He'd left Fleur with my mom and took off." I can't bear to tell her yet about the one-word goodbye note nor his confession of a two-year affair.

"Oh my gosh, Kira, why didn't you say something?"

Because I don't want to admit what a loser I am?

"Well, you were all so happy, and there was so much work to do. I'm trying not to think about it." At least I'm not a total liar.

I cry a little more, which makes Michele cry a little more. She's such a good friend, not being mad at me for ruining her big day.

The prince and princess recess down the aisle, beaming with happiness. Serious perfection. Michele, for all her naiveté and innocence, understands what makes a beautiful bride. "Dang, Vanilla, I know I've told you before, but you deserved to win. You did an incredible job."

The happy couple is out of the cathedral, and we wait for our turn to exit. I have got to pull myself together. I brush the last of the tears from my eyes. "Okay, enough of that. Good riddance to bad rubbish, and all that crap."

The line finally starts to move, though at a snail's pace. I hate receiving lines. They're awkward. I never know what to say. And, I've been with most of the wedding party over the last three days. Doing fittings and alterations requires you getting up close and personal with the model—or bridesmaid—so I've been up in their business. Once you hold someone's boob, making small talk isn't the easiest.

Michele's got to do an interview for the show after the ceremony. I'm spent. I don't want to be around people anymore. That's why I like sewing. Just me, alone in my room. I hate people.

Well, not really but I have limited tolerance for them, and right now I'm at my limit. If I want to be civil tonight, which I have to be, I need a break.

Back in the suite, I take off my dress and peel off the stockings. Royal protocol dictated the use of pantyhose. Michele, being just that much younger than me, was horrified. Me, being of the pasty-leg sort, was okay with it. Twelve years of Catholic school makes a girl accustomed to having to wear pantyhose. On the other hand, they're no less irritating than when I was in high school.

I put on the plush cotton robe provided for guests. Seriously, this place is nicer than the nicest hotel I've ever stayed in (which, for the record is The Pfister in Milwaukee, which tells you the extent of my travels). It's mid-afternoon here, which means early morning back home. I've enough time to Skype with Fleur and still take a little nap before the reception.

"Mommy! I miss you! When are you coming home?"

I cannot let her see me cry. After the first initial meltdown at my mom's—the one that lasted three days—I vowed she would never see me shed another tear over Stan again.

"In a few days, baby. I got to see a real princess today, but she's nowhere near as special as you are."

Fleur continues to tell me about the ongoing saga with her dolls. Apparently they aren't getting along, something about not sharing the kickball at recess. She's learned a lot in pre-K this year. I can only imagine how serious it'll get when she starts kindergarten in the fall. My mom's face appears on the screen behind her.

"Everything okay?" She knows what I mean. I'm worried that Fleur is going to start acting up, which she deserves to do. I told my mom to be on the lookout for it.

"Everything's good. She's had a good week, but she really does miss you."

"Thanks again for everything, Mom. I don't know what I'd do without you."

"You can wipe my butt when I'm old."

I cringe at that mental picture and say my goodbyes.

I've still got a little time to nap before I have to put myself together for the reception. I hear a knock on the outside door. I wonder if Michele ordered food or something. Although we're in the palace, our wing is basically being run like a hotel for the guests of the wedding. From the other side of my door I hear a loud—I mean *loud*—squeal. For the life of me, I can't imagine why Michele would be making such a noise, so I open the door a sliver to take a peek.

I see Michele and her new boyfriend, Lincoln, in a passionate embrace. I close the door to give them their privacy. Not sure what he's doing here, but good for them. I still wonder how she ended up with him instead of Asher. Now with him here, I'm not sure I'll get those details. Bummer.

Although I doubt sleep will come, it does descend quickly and deeply. It feels like five minutes later when I hear a knocking on my door.

"Kira? Are you up? It's time to get ready."

"Five more minutes, Mom."

"Mom?"

The voice isn't right, and it startles me to a more awake state. "Michele?"

"That's better." There's laughter in her voice. I remember about her guest, and it doesn't take much to figure out why she's so happy.

"I'm up and moving. When are we going?"

"About forty-five minutes. Does that give you enough time?"

Stretching out, I take a quick mental survey of what I have to do. Just having to get me ready—it's a novel concept. Normally, I'm getting Fleur ready, egging Stan to get a move on, and then throwing myself together at the last minute. Forty-five minutes on me—I'm not even sure it'll take that long.

"Shouldn't be a problem. I'll come out when I'm done."

I use the bathroom and survey my hair. All it needs is some freshening up with the flat iron. The long layers show off the different colors. Once I straighten it out, I step back. That only took about five minutes. Maybe I could try putting it up. It won't kill me to go a little more glam for such a swanky event.

I bend over at the waist, flipping all my hair forward. Starting at the base of my neck, I French braid the hair up the back of my head, ending with a ponytail on the top of my crown. I twist and pin that into a bun, tucking stray ends in with bobby pins. I loosen up the top to give it a little volume and then spray it into place. Elegant effect achieved. Plus, I love braiding my hair. It shows off the colors even better.

Now onto the makeup. Since Fleur was born, putting my face on in the morning has certainly taken a backseat. Knowing that I needed to look my best, the day before I left for Montabago, I visited Sephora and got myself not only a tutorial in how to make up my face, but also a mortgage payment's worth of makeup. Better to spend Stan's money while I still have it.

I'm not sure I remember everything the heavily made-up clerk taught me, but I do my best. Unfortunately, my best is not good enough. The foundation is okay. I'm skipping the highlighting and contouring. The eyes are not working so well though. My attempt to create a smoky eye turns out much more like a punch in the eye. I wipe it off, touch up the foundation, and start over. And over.

After the third time, I give up. Maybe Michele can help me. Dashing into the living room, I call for her. "Please, for the love of God, help me! I can't do a smoky eye!"

Michele emerges from her room, fully dressed. She looks absolutely stunning.

"I even went to Sephora, and now I can't do it. It looks like I got punched every time I try." I may be starting to panic. It's not every day you go to a royal wedding reception.

Michele, thankfully, knows her way around eye shadow, and before I know it, my lids are properly colored with greens and golds on the top and purple on my lower lash line. She adds the perfect cat eye liner to make my eyes stand out without being overly dramatic. She steps back to admire her handiwork.

"Holy crap, Kira. You look so smokin' hot right now. And you're not even dressed yet. I can't even."

"I can't even" is Michele's favorite phrase. She frequently can't even.

"You look gorgeous yourself. Did you redo your hair?"

She appears to blush. "Actually, Lincoln fixed it for me. It was only fair, after he messed it up. But can you believe it?" She twirls so I can see the full effect.

"I've never seen a straight man who can do that with hair. He is straight, isn't he?"

She giggles and blushes. "Oh yes, totally."

"And when did he get here?" Like I don't already know, but I don't want Michele thinking I was eavesdropping on their escapades like a total creeper.

Again with the giggles. "This afternoon. I can't believe he flew halfway around the world to surprise me!"

As if he knows we're talking about him, which he probably does, since the suite isn't that big, Lincoln pokes his head in the bathroom. "Ladies, we should plan on leaving in about ten minutes."

I take that as my cue to head back and get my dress on. Obviously, the first layer is the Spanx. I've got this one-piece contraption that looks like it's straight out of a late-80s Madonna video. It's like a combination of bike shorts and a long-line bra all in one. Since I'm covered from my boobs to my knees, there's a trap door in the crotch so I can take care of my business. I probably shouldn't drink too much, because I can almost guarantee working the trap door is going to take dexterity I won't possess later in the night.

Once I'm stuffed in like a sausage, I try to arrange the fat rolling out the top of the strapless bra so it looks like cleavage, not that I need any more of that. Now it's time for the dress. It was so perfect for my hair that I couldn't resist, even though it's more body con than I normally wear. The top is a light teal blue satin that is wrapped around one arm to look like a short sleeve and then drapes across the bodice. It's the same color light teal sequin fabric that ombres down into silver, hugging my ample curves. It even has a small train in the back. I finish off the gorgeous creation with amethyst colored shoes and jewelry to compliment my hair.

I take one quick moment to admire myself in the mirror. Eat your heart out, Stan. I'm gorgeous.

Kathryn R. Biel

Chapter 6

At least the food is good. Good's not even the right word. It's out of this world. It is what I imagine is served in Heaven. I can't even identify most of what I'm eating, but it doesn't matter. My tongue is in paradise with the rich flavors layered in complex precision. My Spanx will be demanding overtime pay.

There's plenty of Champagne too. The real stuff, from the Champagne region of France, not the eight-dollar-a-bottle knockoff that I normally buy. Leaning over to Michele, I whisper, "I don't know that I'll ever be able to drink the cheap stuff anymore. This may have ruined me for good."

She holds up her flute, and we clink them together in a little toast. We've done that quite a bit. This is at least my fifth glass. The issue is that, despite the excellent food, this reception is, well, boring. It's not like an American wedding where there's dancing and laughter and loud conversation. This is a reserved function. The dancing has started, but it's formal waltzes and foxtrots. Now, I watch *Dancing with the Stars* with unwavering dedication, but that doesn't

40

mean I can move like that. Not to mention I've no one to dance with.

There's no mingling. No chance to pick up an eligible member of European nobility for my rebound. Stifling a yawn, I look around the enormous room. Most of the other wedding guests look as bored as I feel, and few are doing anything to mask it. I do notice quite a few people looking in my direction. I'm used to it—the stares, the whispers. My hair attracts attention wherever I go. The funny thing is that having brightly colored hair is so part of who I am now that I don't notice it. But others certainly do.

Let's face it, considering the energy level of this crowd, my hair is probably the wildest thing they've ever seen. Michele and Lincoln go out to dance, and I take the opportunity to use the bathroom.

Whoops, I'm a little more tipsy than I thought. I stumble a bit, my heel caught in the fabric of my dress. In an effort to look nonchalant, I smooth my dress down over my legs as I try to recover. Stupid train. I'm not used to wearing this sort of fancy getup. Obviously. I'm used to jeans or leggings when I'm feeling frisky. I do not belong here. I might just head back up to my room.

Stupid night. Stupid expectations. Stupid me.

I don't know why I thought getting all dolled up and attending something way out of my class would make me feel better. Instead I feel worse. Besides Michele and Lincoln, and not counting a brief smile from Princess Maryn, no one has spoken to me. Spoken about me, sure. But not to me. I might as well be invisible.

Yeah, so there's my Debbie Downer Psych 101 rationale for my hair. Without it, I'm completely and totally forgettable. My theme song might as well be "Mr. Cellophane" from Chicago. I'm so unremarkable that even my husband forgot he was married to me.

I snag another flute of the golden nectar on my way out of the ball room. Might as well take advantage of living the royal life while I can. I'll probably be on public assistance once I get home.

"Kira. Kira! Wait up!"

I turn, this time managing to keep my balance, and see Michele chasing after me.

"Yeah, I think I'm outta here. I'm just sitting there getting drunk. I could be sleeping."

"No, that's why I wanted to catch up to you. We want to leave too. There's a town not far from here. We have a car and driver we can use. Supposedly, there's a lot of action there tonight, with everyone celebrating the royal wedding."

"Somebody's got to be celebrating somewhere. This is the most boring wedding I've ever been to. If the food hadn't been positively orgasmic, I would have left hours ago."

From behind me, I hear a strangled little choking noise. The look on Michele's face tells me all I need to know. I just made a huge faux pas in front of someone I shouldn't have. Slowly, filled with dread, I turn to look over my shoulder.

Yup. I might as well stick one of my stilettos in my mouth.

"Um, I'm so sorry, Your Highness. I didn't mean that. I'm not myself right now and—"

"Oh, no, you're right. This is positively dreadful. As much as I love Stephan, I'm afraid the rest of my life is going to be like this. This should be the happiest day of my life, and it was until this started. Now I simply want to go home and go to bed."

Michele tries to soothe her and assure the princess that it's not that bad. "I'm sure, as far as these things go, this is one of the best."

That doesn't help. The princess looks on the verge of tears.

"Seriously, it's not this event. I mean, it's the best food I've ever had. It's more that I feel out of my element and that, well, my husband left me when I got home from the show, and it's hard for me to see how blissfully happy you are."

"So, it's not me, it's you." She's smiling again. Mission accomplished.

"According to Stan, yes. So, I hope you'll forgive me if I don't stay the whole night. I don't want to be a damper."

The princess gives both Michele and me hugs. "I can't thank you both enough for everything you've done." She looks down at her gown. "I still can't believe that you've created this. I had to sit for a royal portrait today. Me—in a royal portrait. It still doesn't seem real. I'm a princess!"

Princess Maryn holds herself so regally that it's easy to forget that she wasn't always part of the royal family. She was a commoner and met Prince Stephan while she was studying at university. She had to be made a duchess in order to be able to get married.

She bids us farewell and moves on, leaving Michele and me standing there. "Yeah, that could have gone better. I'll be keeping my thoughts to myself from now on."

"Bad timing, that's all. Don't sweat it. But this is totes boring. Let's get outta here. I'll go grab Lincoln."

"I'll hit the bathroom and meet you back here. I hope the next venue is better."

I manage to navigate my undergarments with only minor difficulties and meet Michele and Lincoln. A sleek black sedan awaits us out front. I don't think I'll ever get used to someone opening doors for me. It's slightly off-putting, having to wait for someone to do that. The etiquette instructions I received included not opening my own doors. I wish they had included not insulting the princess on her wedding day. Apparently I needed to be told that.

Sliding across the smooth leather seats, it takes a moment to register that there's already someone in the back of the limo.

"Look at you, foxy momma!"

"Holy crap!" It takes me a minute to place the voice and for my heart to return from my throat. "Tony? What are you doing here?"

"Like I was going to miss my cousin's big day?"

"Then why didn't we see you earlier, at the wedding?"

He grins. "Not buying it?"

"Not even close."

"Maybe I came to see you again."

"Not buying that one either." I get that Tony is Michele's cousin, and they're pretty close. He's also Lincoln's roommate, but it still doesn't explain why he's here in Montabago. "No, really. What are you doing here?"

"Does a discounted trip to Europe and break from a soul-sucking job seem more plausible?"

"Definitely. And how is your job soul-sucking? You're like, eighteen. Have you even been working for a year? It takes at least a year to have your soul sucked out."

"I'm twenty-five, thank you very much. I can't help that I was gifted with boyish charm. And I've been in my job for two years, and I barely have any soul left."

We don't get to finish this, as Michele and Lincoln slide in beside us.

"Tony! What are you doing here?"

"I came for your big day."

Michele laughs. "Nice try. What—you get cheap tickets and wanted a break from your soul-sucking job?"

"You do know me, cuz. I figured Lincoln would have tons of down time with you being all wedding-y, and he'd want some company. Oh, and I had miles I had to use. Plus, I haven't tried the European market for ladies. I hear it's quite promising."

"Let's hope the male market is as promising," I mutter. As soon as it's out of my mouth, I hope it wasn't loud enough for anyone to hear.

"Holla sister! We're gonna find a nice European hottie for you tonight!" Michele lifts up her hand for me to high five. I've got no choice but to slap her hand.

Tony looks from Michele to me and then back again. "Um, okay." His right eyebrow lifts ever so slightly. I've always wanted to be able to do that. The look on his face has swiftly changed from jovial to something more serious.

Michele sees it too and looks back at me. Her eyebrow cocks as well. She's asking me permission. I've had a little too much to drink already, but it doesn't stop me from picking up another flute and draining it quickly. I hold up my empty glass. "I'm back on the market, and I'm getting me some tail tonight!"

Chapter 7

Perhaps it was a bit premature to announce that I was in the mood to begin my life as a single woman. Apparently, Tony took that as a personal invitation. He'd been flirty like this before—also in a limo—but at least then I could chalk his behavior up to innocent trifling. With my announcement that I was looking to hook up, how do I say no?

I mean, obviously, I can say no. Do I *want* to say no? For a young whippersnapper, he is pretty attractive. Make that fairly attractive. Okay, he's sort of hot, if I can get past the decade age difference. No, I need to at least wait to see what's available at the bar. I don't know why I think it will be as easy to pick up a guy as it is to order a drink. Perhaps it's all the liquid courage I've imbibed. Any way you look at it, I'm gonna get me some tonight.

Oh jeez, now I sound like a complete and total floozy. I can't just go and get me some with a stranger. I mean, I did that once when I was in college, but that was literally last century. I've been off the market so long—I have no idea where the market even is.

Okay, I need to calm down. I'm not talking about a lifetime commitment here. I only want a little action to remind me that I am valuable and attractive to members of the opposite sex. That's not too much to ask for, is it?

"Earth to Kira. Come in Kira." Michele's waving her hands in front of my face.

"Oh, yeah. What? Huh?"

"We're here. Are you getting out?" The fact that the car had stopped and the doors were open totally escaped me. Man, I'm messed up.

I hustle out of the car, probably moving more like a linebacker than a debutante. Certainly, despite my fancy duds, no one's going to mistake me for a refined member of society.

The air in the bar is thick with a haze of smoke, which I've heard is a typically European thing. I'd forgotten what this was like, and it brings me back to my college days, my hair reeking of smoke after a night out. I haven't smoked in years, but it sort of makes me want a cigarette now. That is, until I see Michele's face crinkle in disgust. "Ugh. I don't know if I can stay here. I, like, can't breathe."

Lincoln coughs a little. "Oh, come on, it's not that bad. Plus, when else are we going to get to do this?"

Even though we've only been in the bar for a few minutes, we're garnering a lot of attention. With Michele and me in our gowns, Lincoln in his tux, and Tony in a suit, it's obvious we were at the wedding.

People start approaching our little group, offering drinks and cheers to the new royal couple. With their thick accents, they ask if we were, indeed, at the wedding, and are amazed and floored when I tell them that Michele is the royal designer. The attention shifts to her, and I can't help but smile.

This is why I came here. To support my friend. This is why it was okay to leave my daughter. This is how I'll get over my marriage falling apart. Or this is how I run away so I can delay facing reality. Same difference.

I try to focus as I scan the bar for someone who looks remotely interesting, but my attention keeps being drawn back to the man standing next to me. With the added height of my heels, we're standing eye to eye. And they're nice brown eyes. Kind brown eyes. Sexy brown eyes.

Ah, what the heck. You only live once, right?

I let my body sag slightly into Tony. "Michele's done wonderful, hasn't she?"

I'm an idiot. If I'm trying to flirt, why am I bringing up another woman? Granted, it's his cousin and I don't think he's into that sort of thing, but still. I've got no game.

He leans in and whispers into my ear. I can't really hear him over the din of the bar.

"What?"

He says something again, his breath hot against my cheek. I can't help but tilt my head, showing him more of my neck. I still can't make out what he's saying. I take another sip of my drink while I ponder if I can say "what" again. My socially awkward pause must clue him into the fact that I have no idea what he's saying. Why is the music so loud in here?

Tony takes my arm just above the elbow and starts to steer me toward the door. Maybe I'm more drunk than I realize, and he's going to send me home. Obviously my ears don't work anymore. Once outside, he turns me to face him. We're eye to eye.

"Are you okay?"

That's what he was saying? That's it?

"Um, yeah. Fine." I try to act nonchalant. I'm not much of an actor.

"No, really. Are you okay? What happened?"

"What do you mean?" I know exactly what he means. Obviously, it's the last thing I want to talk about right now.

"Last time I saw you, you were brutally rebuffing my flirtation, because you're married."

"Lucky for you, that's no longer the case." And I give him a smile. A slow, sweet smile.

"What happened?"

"I don't want to talk about it tonight. In fact, I want to talk about anything but. Let's talk about you. Let's talk about the weather. Let's talk politics." Apparently my attempts to be flirty and seductive are falling flat.

He cocks his head slightly as he looks deep into my eyes. I can't hold his gaze and look down. With a light hand under my chin, he lifts my face back up. "I just want to make sure you know what you're doing."

"I want to feel wanted. In this moment, right here and right now. I want to feel pretty and sexy and desired. That's all I want."

Now it's his turn to smile a slow, sexy grin. "Are you sure?"

"Do you meet that criteria?"

He pulls me in closer; my body presses into his. His desire is evident. With his lips millimeters from mine, "You are the most stunning, vibrant, sexy thing I've ever seen."

And then his lips are on mine. The kiss is slow and sweet at first, but quickly deepens. I haven't kissed another man in fifteen years. Tony feels different. Not wrong. Different. New. Exciting. A small moan escapes me as I pull him tighter to me. My hands are in his hair and he's moving his hands over my bottom.

And we're still outside the bar. This is not going to work.

Pulling apart slightly, I'm breathless. "We need to go. Now."

"I'll get the driver."

"What about Michele and Lincoln?"

"I'm not really into the group thing. Plus, I'm related to Michele, so that's pretty icky."

He makes me laugh. "Michele has an issue with the group thing too. Must be a family trait."

"I don't even want to know why you know that about my cousin."

"I'll let her tell you that. And for the record, I've been in a monogamous relationship for the past fifteen years."

"Check please! Let's blow this Popsicle stand. I'll send the car back for them. They won't miss us at all."

We scurry off to the waiting limo. Once in the back, I don't know what to do. I mean, it's obvious what we're about to do. Do we start now? Go at it in the back of the limo like horny teenagers? I mean, this isn't prom. We can't be tearing off each other's clothes as we enter the palace. So instead I sit there, up in my own head, worrying and fretting.

"If you don't want this, it's okay." Tony nudges me slightly. We're sitting close together, shoulder to shoulder. I look at my hands, clenched tightly in my lap.

I turn to him and smile. "No, I do want this. I'm trying to convince myself that we can contain ourselves and not start going at it in the car."

He slides an arm around my shoulders and pulls me into him. "I've been trying to convince myself of the same thing. You're absolutely stunning tonight. I keep thinking about all the things I want to do to you."

His words send tingles down my ... everywhere. Luckily, the limo pulls to a stop. Alighting the vehicle, I realize we're at Tony's hotel rather than the palace. "Oh, I didn't know we were going here."

"I figured this would give us a little more privacy."

"You think of everything, don't you?"

"I'm trying."

With his arm around me, we hurry through the lobby and into the elevator. The anticipation courses through my body as the bell signals floor after floor. Why does he have to be on the twelfth floor?

If my feet weren't screaming from being trapped in my heels all night, I'd probably sprint down the hall. I glance at Tony. His eyes are hungry, mirroring mine. As we reach his door, he fumbles with the key, inserting the card first one way, and then another.

"I hate these stupid things."

"It's like my cell phone charger. There are only two sides, and I still have to try it three times before I get it right."

"I'm glad I'm not the only one." The green light flashes, and the door swings open.

Let's do this.

Chapter 8

You know how in movies when the couple heads back to the hotel room, ripe with passion, and things flow seamlessly? So not the situation here.

I think the first problem is I'm a little drunk. My feet are screaming in agony from being imprisoned in my stilettos all night, and my control of them is waning. There's some tripping and stumbling. Maybe more than some. Certainly not the epitome of grace and sexiness. My fine-motor skills leave a bit to be desired as I fumble with the buttons on Tony's shirt, which makes me get the giggles. And once I get the giggles, it's hard for me to stop.

Oh Lord, this is not going well.

He smiles in amusement at me but doesn't share in my laughter. That is until it's his turn to undress me.

Because I've totally forgotten about the contraption I'm wearing under my gown to smooth out my nooks and crannies. Tony's holding me in an embrace, reaching around me to slide the zipper down.

His skills are so much smoother than mine. With a swift move, he pushes the dress off my shoulder and down my body. Revealing the lingerie from hell.

There's nothing sexy about being stuffed into Spanx, with my rolls spilling over the top. I look like an overstuffed sausage. The crotch trapdoor has busted open and my lady bits are half hanging out, but not in a good way. To make matters worse (as if it could get worse), it's not even a sexy black, but the ever-practical nude color.

Tony steps back.

"What the heck is that?" His eyes are darting up and down my body. I glance down. I even have a fat bulge at the bottom of the shorts. Cripes, even my knees have a muffin top! "Are you going scuba diving?"

And then, horror among horrors, he starts laughing. Not just amusement, but a full-on, hold-your-belly laugh.

Oh my God, I want to die right now. Please put me out of my misery.

Because my mortification isn't complete, I burst into tears. Absolute waterworks, ugly cry. Sobs wrack my body, and I can't control it. Tony stands there for a minute, most likely terrified at the spastic display of disaster that he brought back to his hotel room.

Gingerly, he sits down on the bed next to me where I've crumpled into a puddle. "Kira, I'm so sorry. I don't know ... well, crap. I'm sorry." He places his hand lightly on my back. "I'm an idiot."

Whereas a few minutes ago his touch made me tingle, now it's making my skin crawl. "Please don't touch me." He withdraws his hand in compliance. Now I feel cold and empty. And maybe like I'm going to hurl a little bit. Not necessarily from the drinking, although that certainly doesn't help.

This is my life. Alone and fat. Not fat but chubby, at least. Having men laugh at me. Leave me.

Springing from the bed, I grab the gown still pooled at my feet and cover my hideousness. With it not even fully on, I march toward the door and exit. Once in the elevator, I get myself covered and take off my shoes. The concierge looks at me like I've got three heads as I scurry across the lobby.

"Can you please help me?"

"Certainly, ma'am. With what do you need assistance?"

I'm so glad they speak English here. "I need to leave." I also need to stop crying so that they don't transport me to the insane asylum instead. "Where would you like to go, ma'am? Do you need special assistance?"

"I need to go to the royal palace. I'm a guest there."

"Mmm. The palace is not open to the public."

"Yes, I realize that, but that's where I'm staying. I was at the wedding."

"I'm afraid there's no way to get on the grounds."

"Isn't there a guard or something? Can't they let me in?"

"Do you have identification on you?"

I don't know why I do this, but I pat my legs and rear, as if looking for a wallet stuffed in my back pocket. I had a small clutch at some point in the night. I don't even know where that is. "No, I've misplaced my purse." Where is that stupid thing?

"Then where would you like to go?"

Sigh. This is going to take a while. "I need to go to the palace. I'm a guest of Michele Nowa ... Noka .... Um, I don't remember her last name." Michele's last name is something Polish, but I really can't say that, can I? "But she designed the wedding gown. I helped." I sound like Baby in *Dirty Dancing*. I might as well have said that I carried a watermelon.

"So you're a guest of a guest, and you don't know that guest's name?" He's looking at me like I'm nuts. If there's a silent alarm under the counter, it wouldn't surprise me if he's triggering it right now. "Ma'am, could you please tell me what you are doing in this hotel?"

"I came here with a ... friend. We had a fight, and I'd rather not be here anymore."

"Well, I'm afraid there's nothing I can do for you."

I have nothing on me. No phone. No money. No information to get me what I need to pass Go.

Awesome.

What choice do I have but to go back to Tony's room? What if he doesn't open the door for me? What if he laughs at me again? You know, this is all his fault. He was the mean one. Not me. He should take care of me. He'd better.

Here goes nothing.

Knock, knock, knock.

I can't believe my life has come to this. Please wake me from this bad dream that I'm having.

I thought the worst thing in the world would be having to crawl back to Tony and ask him for help after he humiliated me. Nope. Not even close. The worst thing is crawling back only to have him not answer the door.

Fantastic. Shoes in hand, I lean my back against the door and bang my head slightly. I'd no idea I could feel any lower than I did when I found out Stan left me. And cheated on me.

Defeat washes over me as I slide down the door to sit on the floor. This day has stretched on forever, and I just wish I were in my bed. Certainly anywhere but the hotel hallway. Fatigue washes over me as my last remaining energy drains away. I can't wait to get home and forget this night ever happened.

Chapter 9

"Kira. Kira. You've got to wake up."

I swat at the bothersome voice that's pulling me out of my slumber. The voice is also shaking me, and that's pretty annoying as well. "Kira—we've got to get going."

The voice, slowly growing louder, sounds familiar. Why can't I place it? The feel of the bed is off too. Wait—where am I?

Bolting upright, my eyes fly open and then shut as my skull makes hard contact with something equally hard. Stars shoot before my eyes. My hands cover my forehead, trying to rub the pain away.

"Owww! Son of a—" The hard object with which I connected is in as much pain. Good. Because now I recognize the voice.

"What the heck, Tony? What are you doing?"

"Trying to wake you up and not getting much thanks other than a concussion."

My eyes are open now. I'm in Tony's room, in his bed. I have no idea how I got here. I'm not sure I want to know. Well, of course I want to know, because I want plenty of ammunition when I rip him a new one.

"I meant why am I here? How did I get here? Why am I in your bed? I distinctly remember leaving last night." I try to recall more details. Some things are fuzzy. Some things are crystal clear. Those are the things I wish never to remember.

"After you left, I felt horrible. I went to look for you but couldn't find you. I even thought you might be trying to walk, so I walked miles. Then, when I got back to the hotel, there you were, outside my door."

"Oh. I must have fallen asleep." I don't remember. I wish I did. But that doesn't explain how I got in here. And it certainly doesn't explain why my gown is lying across the desk on the other side of the room. I'm afraid to peek under the sheets. What if I'm naked?

I squirm slightly, trying to figure out what's going on. I feel tight fabric around my lower half. It's the garment that simultaneously made me look fantastic and feel foolish all at the same time. At least I'm not naked. There would be so much trouble if I were naked.

But, oh am I pissed. Like, super pissed. What right did he have to get me undressed? Isn't that a violation or something? I hate Tony right now. I think I hate him more than Stan. I didn't even know that was possible.

Clutching the sheet in front of my breasts, which are spilling over the top of the undergarment, I start spluttering and spitting. I can't even put together a coherent thought. Words like "violate," "assault," and a few other choice words spew out.

"Whoa, simmer down." He's stood up, backing away from the bed with his hands in front of him like someone trying to soothe a lion. "I didn't touch you."

"Of course you didn't. You were probably too busy laughing at me."

"Jeez, Kira, I wasn't laughing at you."

"No? Because that's exactly what is seemed like to me."

"That's not what happened. Your perspective is skewed."

"Skewed? *Skewed?* I think it was pretty clear. You've been flirting with me since the moment we met. I made it clear that I was looking for a hook up. You indicated interest. You kissed me. We got back here. There was ... groping. And the minute my dress came off, you started making fun of me and laughing. Now, I know I may have had a bit to drink, but do I have it wrong?"

"Yes."

"Which part?"

"Well ... I, um, ahhh ..."

"That's what I thought." Like something out of a movie, I stand up, ripping the sheet off the bed and dramatically wrapping it around me, toga style.

"I wasn't laughing at you."

"Yes, you were. At least be man enough to admit it." God, I am so angry. And hungover, which doesn't do much to help my mood.

"Okay, I was sort of laughing at you. But not *you.* More that, that ... thing you're wearing. Seriously, what is that?"

"Spanx."

"I didn't think we were at that stage in our relationship."

He'd be dead right now if looks could kill. "And we never will be. They're foundation garments."

"Foundation ... garments?" He rolls the words slowly, like they're in another language.

"Oh, my God. Are you dense or something? They hold my fat in and smooth it all out." He continues to stare at me like I've got three heads. "Like a girdle."

"But that's something old ladies wear. Why would you wear it?"

To quote Michele, I can't even.

I let out an exasperated sigh. "Because I am old and fat. Anything else? If I wear fitted clothes without my Spanx, you can see every bump and ripple and cellulite and all the things I would never want a man I want to sleep with to see. I've been with my husband for the past fifteen years, so he knew. I didn't have to hide it from him."

"Did he think those under-girdle-spanky things were funny too?"

The last thing I want to do is talk about my husband's perception of my body. Or my husband. Ex-husband. Close enough.

"Tony, I need to go. Can I use your phone to call Michele? I don't have any way to get back into the palace otherwise."

He obliges, and hands me his cell. Wanting some privacy, I drag my sheet and head into the bathroom.

"Oh, my God Tony. Do you have Kira with you? She disappeared last night. We have her purse. Did you see her? Do I have to call the police or gendarme or whatever they're called here?"

"Michele, it's me. Calm down."

"Oh thank God. I was totally freaking out."

"I could tell."

"Wait, you're calling from Tony's phone? Does that mean you and he ...? Are we going to be cousins-in-law soon? How was it? What does this mean?"

You'd think I'd be used to a barrage of questions by now. It's Michele's style. She talks a mile a minute and legitimately has ADHD. Most of the time it doesn't bother me. In this moment, however, it's pretty grating. I'm fairly certain I'd be aggravated by a soothing hot bubble bath right now.

"Michele, stop. I can't. I need to be picked up from Tony's hotel. They wouldn't get me a cab to the palace so I had to stay here. I just need to go. Now."

"Um, okay. I'll get a car sent over. Where exactly are you?"

I give her the name of the hotel and disconnect. I don't want to leave the protection of the bathroom. *He's* out there. I don't ever want to see him again. I know, due to my relationship with Michele, I will probably run into him sometime in the future. That thought makes my stomach turn. While in the bathroom, I make use of the facilities. My hair is still up, but it's looking a little—a lot—worse for wear. I try to smooth it down with some water and then wash my face. I re-stuff myself into my Spanx, making sure all my bits and pieces are covered as best they can be. I do a slow turn to see my body from all angles, trying to see myself through Tony's eyes.

Big mistake.

I re-wrap the sheet around my body, trying to cover myself and make it flattering at the same time.

Good thing I'm used to working with fabric. I take a big breath and exit the bathroom.

Tony looks concerned. Good. Let him.

He's laid my dress out on the bed. Next to that, there's a pair of sweatpants and a T-shirt. He sees me looking at them.

"I didn't know if you'd, uh, want to be in something more comfortable."

Someday I might look back on this moment and realize what a sweet gesture he's made, but now is not that time.

"I'll just put the dress on, thanks." I might as well complete the walk of shame. Shame is certainly a good word to describe my mood right now. Snatching the dress off the bed, I march back into the bathroom. No way am I getting undressed in front of him again. Once back in my gown, which now makes me feel fat and ugly, I stomp out of the bathroom and right out of Tony's room without even looking at him. Well, without looking directly at him. A sideways glance tells me that he looks as miserable as I feel. Good.

I manage to keep it together until I step off the elevator in the hotel lobby. The tears start, slow at first, and then bursting forth like the dam broke. I see the palace car and slide in without saying anything. I see the driver glancing back and do my best to ignore him. But even though I keep an aloof posture, I can't help focusing on what he must be thinking. And none of it is favorable.

I'm fortunate to be brought to a side door that leads almost directly to the hall where my room is. Of course Michele and Lincoln are cozied up on the couch, all lovey dovey.

Michele leaps up upon seeing me. "Oh Kira! Are you okay? You look terrible."

"I see you have the same amount of tact as your cousin. It must run in the family."

With that, I storm to my room, slamming the door as hard as I can. It's a nice, heavy oak door, so that slam is pretty satisfying. As hastily as possible, I tear off my dress and Spanx, balling them up and throwing them across the room. I find my most unattractive, comfortable, baggy clothes and put them on. I'd packed these for sleeping in, but I don't care. I might as well look how I feel.

There's a soft knock on the door. "Kira?"

"I don't want to talk."

"Can I come in?"

"I don't want to talk."

The door opens and Michele walks in. Gingerly she closes the door behind her, like I used to when I was sneaking in to check on a sleeping Fleur. Except I'm not sleeping, and I told her I didn't want to talk.

"I said I didn't want to talk." To emphasize my point, I flop face-first on my bed. Michele sits down next to me. Of course she does.

"What happened?"

I know she's going to keep asking until I tell her something, so I might as well. "Nothing happened."

"What? How could nothing have happened? I saw the way the two of you were looking at each other at the bar. And the body language. It was totes hot. What gives? Could he not perform? You know, I think I remember Aunt Maria complaining about that with Uncle Vito once. Maybe it's a familial thing. Not that I want to think about it. Have you ever had a guy have

65

that happen before? I haven't, but I hear that it does. But it's about him, not you. It's not because he doesn't find you attractive, because he does. I know he does."

There were way too many words for me to even process right now.

"No, it wasn't that. He ... well, that wasn't the issue." I know it wasn't. I felt it when our bodies were pressed close together.

"What then? Is he a minute man?"

Oh God, I do not want to be having this conversation.

"No, Michele." I can't keep the exasperation from my voice. I'm too tired and upset and frustrated to be dealing with this right now. "It wasn't that. We didn't have sex."

"What, what? Why not? I thought you were looking to get a little sumthin' sumthin'."

"I was. It didn't work out that way."

"Just tell me why not?"

For a moment, I consider telling her. But how can I? She's my friend, but he's her cousin. She'll try to defend him and tell me what a great guy he is. I don't want to hear it. Maybe, somewhere in the back of my brain, I sort of know he's not as bad as I'm making him out to be, but the majority of my head is screaming that he's the devil incarnate. Or at least the devil's impish little brother. Certainly a relative of Satan to say the least.

"I don't want to get into it. I really don't. Please drop it."

"Fine."

I can't see her face, but I can tell she's pouting. Tough. I'm not going through it again. In fact, I can't wait to get home and never think about this trip again.

Chapter 10

"It's been four months, Kira. You need to get off the couch."

"I do get off the couch, Mom. Every day, whether I want to or not. I take Fleur to school and to dance and to Scouts. I go to work."

"Yeah, but that's it. You mope around all night. Every night. As soon as you get home, you put on those ugly sweatpants, and you mope. I'm sick of the moping."

"I'm not moping. I'm thinking."

"You're moping. And I can't believe I'm going to say this, but for the love of God, would you please do something with your hair? It looks terrible."

"I thought you'd be happy I stopped dying it."

"I thought I would too, but not like this." Mom's flitting around the room, straightening things out. Nothing's out of place, but that doesn't stop her. Sort of like when she dusts, and there's no trace of dust. I used to like to dust when I could write my name in it. That way, I felt more productive. "The color that's left is all faded and, well, gross. And your real hair is ... I don't know. It's bad."

"Thanks, Mom. Do you want to call me fat too?"

"Well, now that you mention it, your diet's been pretty unhealthy, and you've been relatively inactive."

I know she's trying to be supportive. She's goading me into doing something. And even though I know what she's doing, I take the bait.

"Fine. Can you watch Fleur tomorrow night? I'm going to go out after work."

"Tomorrow's my Bunco night. And I thought Stan had her this weekend."

"No, he cancelled. Again." In the four—almost five—months since we've been separated, I think he's seen Fleur twice. I never expected this out of him, but, then again, I never expected him to walk out on me and shack up with a twenty-year-old. Which means she was barely legal when they met. At least he didn't trade me in for someone older. And at least, so far, he's been paying child support.

"Fine. I can get a sub for Bunco. It's at Maude's house, and she serves the worst snacks. I get heartburn every time."

The divorce was quick and easy. I'm waiting on the paperwork to make it final. Hopefully that comes in soon. He gave me a decent financial settlement, because he took all the physical possessions. I mean, seriously, who does that?

I can't afford to buy all new stuff, so I'm still with my mom. Considering the amount of help I need with Fleur, it seems to be for the best. Except my mom is right, though I don't want her to know I know that. I need to stop moping. I'm totally moping around.

My co-workers at House of Crafts are doing karaoke tomorrow night. They do it every Thursday.

And I'm invited every Thursday. I never go, because I'm moping. As of this moment, I need to mope no more.

I pull my body off the couch and head to my room. I also know she's right about the hair. Frantically, I text Emay, my hairdresser, to see if she can squeeze me in. That's sort of laughable considering it can take up to six hours to get a good rainbow or unicorn look going. That's what I call my look when I have a bunch of colors in it. While I wait for her reply, I head to the closet to see what I should wear.

I'm not going to pick anybody up. Heck no. Not after the disaster in Montabago. But I want to look good. For me. I want to feel good. Nothing in the closet appeals to me.

I find my going out jeans and try them on, nervous that I won't be able to button them. Except the opposite is true. They're loose. Take that, Mom! My weight is down, not that you can tell in the baggy sweats that are my uniform. Weight loss is usually good, but it makes the jeans super-unflattering. The last thing I need is a droopy butt.

I reach into the depths of the closet to find that one last bag of clothes I didn't unpack. My Martin Luther King bag—so named because I've always had a dream that someday I'd fit into them. Hot diggity dog, the size ten jeans fit. They're a big ten, but I'm not going to focus on that.

I can't go out topless. I mean I could, but I think they frown upon that, at least at the onset of the night. Since my closet has returned no answers, I do the next best thing. I pull out my bag of fabric and settle on a purple jersey knit. There's a wide lace the same shade. Perfect. I take out my sewing machine and set it up on Mom's dining room table. A few hours later, my back is sore from bending over, and my eyes are tired, but I've got a chill, sexy off-the-shoulder top. My amethyst shoes would go perfect, but I don't know if I can bring myself to wear them again. I'll think about it.

Emay texted me back and is coming in early to see me right after Fleur goes to school. I have to work at noon, so it'll be tight, but doable. I'll have her do the roots teal and wash that color through. Some of the variation in color will still be visible, even though it won't be that prominent. At least it will look better than it does now. It should take less time than doing all four colors again.

I can't believe I'm going through all of this just to go out for karaoke. On the other hand, I have let myself go a little. Well, a lot. I need to do something fun. And this should be fun.

My co-workers, Jani and Morris, are shocked when I stroll into work with freshly done hair and plans for debauchery. Not exactly debauchery but letting loose a little. I am in desperate need of fun. Jani and Morris are quite entertaining and make me laugh in the course of our typical workday, cutting and stacking and folding fabrics.

Jani's fluttering around, dancing and singing in light of my news. I'm not sure I can handle this sustained energy level until I leave at four. I don't make much working at House of Crafts. It's above minimum wage, so that's good. When I'm there (ten to four most weekdays and every other weekend), I manage the fabric department. I was told I was massively overqualified to work there, but I was desperate and so were they. In all honesty, it's helpful to have someone who can answer sewing questions.

I've needed a job where I could use my knowledge but that wasn't too stressful. I keep hoping that surrounding myself with all the material will get my creative juices flowing again. Until last night when I made that shirt, I haven't sewn a thing since I left the contest. I've got no motivation. No drive. My well is dry.

I hate that Stan stole this from me. It's not fair. But today, I'm starting over. I'm going to find out who I am now, and what I want from life.

The problem is, I have no idea.

And as much as I want to blame Stan, part of the problem is me. I don't want to go back to retail. My brief stint as a buyer wasn't bad, but it wasn't what I wanted either. I welcomed the chance to be home with Fleur. When the auditions for the show came about, I never figured I even had a chance. I certainly didn't want to tell anyone what I was doing. I brought my audition pieces in garbage bags, lest Stan question why I needed so many suitcases for a three-day trip.

I don't think anyone thought the girl with green hair and black trash bags would be a contender. Most of all me. That I looked like such a long shot but still made the cut should fill me with confidence. But instead, I've let myself become completely derailed. At this point, I'm considering simply buying pre-made patterns to get myself back in the habit. And even that would be something.

Hey, look at me. Thinking about the future. Making plans. Trying to motivate myself. Go me.

"So, what's his name?" Jani slides up next to me behind the fabric counter. There's a lull between customers, so I'm taking the opportunity to fold and markdown the leftover remnants.

"What's whose name?" I have no idea what she's talking about. All of the customers on this Friday morning have been middle-aged-to-old ladies, except for a handful of young moms with screaming toddlers.

"Your man."

"What man?"

"You come in today, your hair's all done, and you're finally going out with us tonight. And I heard you tell a customer that you made a shirt last night. I've never known you to actually make anything. I know you talk about sewing a lot, but I didn't think you could actually sew."

"I graduated from Columbus School of Design. I was a contestant on *Made for Me!*" My voice is rising. I can sew rings around my co-workers.

"Yeah, that's what the rumors are, but you, like never do anything. You don't even touch the fabric."

I know what she means. I've spent hours in my life walking past bolts of fabric, letting it run through my fingers. Experiencing the texture with my fingers. Letting my brain explore through my hands. She's right—I don't do that anymore.

"I got a bit burnt out on the show. And you know that I've had some personal things." I haven't shared tons with my co-workers.

"What personal things?"

I might as well share. "When I arrived home from filming, my husband had left me. He cleared out the house and was gone. Apparently, he moved on. About two years ago."

"Right, so who's the new man?"

"There isn't anyone. Why would you think that?"

Jani sighs and rolls her eyes. "All the stuff I already said. Plus, today's the first day you're not wearing your ring."

I look down. She's right. I took my rings off last night while sewing. I never wear jewelry, lest I snag the fabric. But this time I didn't put them back on. What surprises me most is that I didn't miss them.

"My mom yelled at me for moping around."

"Were you?"

"Yeah, I guess."

"So ... that's it?"

I shrug. "Yeah, pretty much. She was right. I needed to get off the couch and do something. And that started with making plans and fixing my hair. That's it. No man."

"Oh, dang. I thought for sure there had to be someone. A woman?"

I laugh. "Nope. Not that. I got off the couch for me."

Jani's mouth hangs agape. She's only about twenty-two, and is chronically in one relationship or another. I don't know that she's been single since she hit puberty. The thought of doing something for yourself rather than for a man is way beyond her. I do hope she gets there someday, although I fear she won't.

"So, tonight, our mission is to find you a man."

"I don't want a man." I can't help but shudder at the thought of how that went last time I was on a mission to find a man.

"A woman?"

"No, and please stop asking. I don't want anyone right now."

"Awww, come on. You've got to get back on that horse someday."

How do I tell her that I already tried and fell off? And that after I fell off, the horse pooped on me. No, thanks. I'm good.

Chapter 11

Morris is belting out "Don't Stop Believing," and the crowd is going wild. It's hard not to, since he's got a fabulous voice. And stage presence to boot. He's so funny. Going out with Morris and Jani is now the highlight of my week. It's the third week in a row I've done this. They're like the odd couple. Jani's Latin temperament makes her quick to action and slow in reason. She's young, feisty, and never lets anyone forget it. Morris, on the other hand, is a middle-aged, self-proclaimed queen. He dabbles in drag but enjoys going out as a male as well. He's surprisingly laid back. The drama only comes out when he's got his wig and full makeup on. According to him at least. I've yet to see him dressed up.

I feel my phone buzzing in the pocket of my size ten jeans. Yes, I'm going to keep saying that because I feel so darn good about it. Although, truth be told, since I've returned to the land of the living, so has my appetite. And the pants are starting to feel a bit snug again. Whatever. I don't care. I'm not starving myself for what the label on the inside of my clothes says. Life's too short not to eat dessert.

Once I extract my phone, I see that Michele's texted me about four times. The messages start out with the normal greetings and then progress into the real reason for her texting. As I'm reading, more texts keep coming in. The upshot is that she got a slew of orders on her Etsy store. It makes me a bit jealous. If I could make her clothes for her, I wouldn't have to think. I could just sew her stuff.

This is definitely something I'll have to consider mentioning to her. Ask her if she needs help. Since my creative juices have dried up, it would be a way to get back into the swing a bit more. Chances are she'd pay more than House of Crafts too. Depending on how much work she has for me, maybe I could keep my hours at the store and sew in the evenings after Fleur's gone to bed. Someday I'd like to move out of my mom's house.

"Kira! It's your turn." Morris is off the stage and sweating profusely. "I need a wipe." I place my phone on the table and pick up a napkin to hand to him. Delicately, he dabs the top of his balding head with it. "What are you doing tonight?"

"I think I'm going with a little Tay-Tay."

"Ugh, not again."

"What can I say? My daughter loves Taylor Swift. I have limited exposure to music these days." With that, I prance up to the stage and do my best attempts to shake it off.

Now I'm as sweaty as Morris was. My hair is damp and making me even hotter, so I use the ever-present rubber band on my wrist to twist it into a large top knot as I plop back down in my seat. "I think I totally killed it."

Jani glances from me to Morris and back again. It gives me a distinct feeling of unease.

"What?"

Looks are exchanged again. Jani then looks down at her hands. Morris is looking at my phone in the middle of the table. I didn't realize it was there. I pick it up and put it back in my pocket. Neither of my tablemates says anything. Maybe I was flat or sharp or totally off-key, and they're afraid to tell me.

"Was I that bad? I thought it was okay. You'd tell me if it's that bad, right?"

The looks go back and forth again. That's it, I'm out of patience. I'm also out of beer, which may have something to do with my temper. "Just spit it out!"

Jani nervously clears her throat. "Who's Tony?"

Wait—what?

She continues. "Um, your phone went off. It was a text from Michele. She said that Tony wants to call you and can he. So, I may have scrolled through your contacts and found him. He's like hot. Who is he? Why didn't you tell us about him?"

Because I never, ever want to speak of him again?

"He's nobody."

"Honey, that nobody can bring his al dente noodle to my spaghetti house any time."

"What?" I have no idea what he's talking about.

"I'd let him butter my biscuit."

I will not acknowledge this is happening. "Why do you keep talking about food? Are you hungry? Do you want to order something? I need another beer anyway, so flag down the waiter."

"Oh my God, Kira, stop being so obtuse."

"Stop being so nosy." I manage to snag John, our regular waiter, and order another beer.

The next singer comes on, so I turn my back to Jani and Morris. The longer I sit there, the straighter my back becomes and the more my blood boils. How dare they? How dare Michele? How dare Tony?

John returns with my beer, which I drain in one long drink, holding up my finger to him, asking him to wait. Once done, I wipe my mouth with the back of my hand and put the glass down on the table. The gas bubble is already filling my stomach. I manage to croak out, "Another, please."

John cocks his head. "Are you sure? Are you okay?"

"I'm sure, and no, I'm not okay." My stomach's suddenly, and understandably, not feeling so good. The majority of the bar's patrons are between me and the bathroom, so I make the executive decision to head out the front door. There's a good certainty that I'm going to vomit. The cool fall night air hits me. It feels good and makes me feel bad all at the same time. Oh no, this is not good. I bend forward slightly so that I don't mess my shoes. The burp is welling up, making my chest burn. Before I can even think about controlling it, it erupts from my body with a loud, "BRRRRAAAAAAAAP."

I swear I felt that from my toes.

But man, do I feel so much better instantaneously. I don't think I'm even going to hurl anymore. A smile spreads across my face. I'm ready to go back in.

That is, until I hear a slow clapping behind me.

"That was impressive. Like seriously impressive. There was one guy in my frat who could do that, but I think yours might have been better."

My hands fly to my mouth as I see who is giving me the compliment. He's a clean-cut guy in jeans and a Henley. Blond hair. Taller than I am, so that's a good sign. Not too shabby. "Uh, excuse me?" It's all I can think of to say.

"No excusing needed. That was awesome."

"It doesn't usually happen. Perhaps my days of shotgunning should stay in my past. I haven't done that in years."

"Let me guess, it's totally been three years."

I'm flattered that he would think I'm a decade younger than I am. I fall for it hook, line, and sinker. Looking at my shoes, I can't help but twist my feet in a little and blush. I feel like a schoolgirl. "It's been a little more than that, but thanks anyway."

"I'm Ted."

"Kira."

"Tara?"

"No, Kiiiiira." I say it slow, drawing it out in hopes he'll understand. No one ever gets my name right the first time. When I was in college, this is what used to happen all the time. I'd even get phone calls for the most random names. Honestly, the guys didn't even try to come close. That's a big pet peeve of mine and would be the kiss of death for them.

"Kara?"

Oh my God, this is not a good sign. I tell him one last time and he finally gets it right.

"So, Kira, can I buy you a drink?"

My gut clenches again, screaming at me that I'm not ready for this. My heart continues to flutter a little though, flattered by the attention it's been starved for. "Um, I think I may be done drinking, at least for a little while, but you can buy me a water."

"I think the water's free."

"Well, what do you know? I'm a cheap date."

Ted laughs and holds the door for me as we walk back into the bar. I wave at Jani and Morris and follow Ted to the bar. We manage to snag two barstools.

"With lemon or without?"

What a thoughtful guy. "Without is fine."

Ted orders my water and his whiskey. I don't know how old he is, but he's drinking a grown up drink. That's a plus in my book.

It's hard to make conversation over the din in the bar. Some of the singers are good, but some are horrible. Those seem to bring even more noise.

"You gonna take a turn?" Ted nods toward the stage.

"Already did. You missed it. A shame too, because I killed it."

"Oh, so do you do this regularly?" I think I pick up a bit of disdain in his voice. That can't be right. He came to a karaoke bar. Obviously he has to expect that people he meets here will get up and sing. I mean, why else would you come here?

"I've only been a few times. My co-workers," I point to the table where Morris and Jani are trying hard—and failing miserably—not to obviously stare at us, "are into it. It's fun, and I need some fun in my life right about now."

"Well, if this is your idea of fun, then you definitely need to hang out with me, and I'll show you some fun." He pulls his phone out and hands it to me. "Put your number in so I can text you later."

I've been out of the dating scene for a long time. Is this how it's done now? I guess it must be. I put my number in and hand the phone back. Instantly, I feel a buzzing in my back pocket.

"Now you can text me back. I've got to catch up with some friends, but I'll be in touch. I definitely want to get together sometime soon."

Ted stands up, gives me a kiss on the cheek, and leaves the bar. I look over to see Jani and Morris raising their arms in a victory salute.

Who needs Stan? Who needs Tony? I can do this on my own, and frankly, it was pretty dang easy.

Chapter 12

"Fleur, Mommy's going out tonight."

"Again?" Her lower lip sticks out, indicating her displeasure. Secretly, I think it's adorable. I can see her reflection in the mirror as I French braid one of her pigtails.

"I haven't been out since last week."

"I feel like we never get to hang out anymore."

This is what I get from a five-year-old. How do you argue with that?

Ted's texted me a few times throughout the week. We'd tentatively set up plans to hang out tonight, although I am still waiting for him to confirm.

"How 'bout tomorrow; we'll do something special, just you and me?"

"It's always just you and me. When's Daddy coming back?"

I sigh and count to ten. Again. We go through this at least once a week. It's taking everything in my power not to call Stan every name in the book. The bad ones that is. I will not be that woman. I will not be that woman.

"I don't know. And when he does come back, it's to see you because he loves you."

"Why doesn't he love you anymore?"

I wish I knew.

"Sometimes it happens between mommies and daddies, but it doesn't mean that how we feel about you will change." Even as I say it, I know it's not true. I guess things weren't how I wanted to think they were.

"Let's think about what fun we're going to have tomorrow. What do you want to do?" I stick my hand out, and she gives me a pink hair elastic that I fasten around her little braid.

"I want to do it tonight. Can't you go out tomorrow instead?"

I move to the other side of her head. Unlike her father, nothing is more important to me than my daughter. "Okay, I'll reschedule." If Ted doesn't like it, then it wasn't meant to be. Fleur comes first. Always.

"Good. Can we watch *Frozen*?"

She's seen it about a million times already, meaning I've seen it at least five hundred thousand. The worst part is that I end up with "Let It Go" in my head for days. Since I don't have Idina Menzel's range, I can't belt it out without cats shrieking in pain and glass shattering.

"Sure. And we should probably plan on painting our nails."

That's all the reassurance she needs, and my work here is done. So's her hair, and we head to the kitchen to get breakfast. I'll text Ted after she leaves.

****

"Are you ready for tonight? What are you wearing? Are you excited?" Jani's hitting me with a barrage of questions before I can even punch in.

"Yeah, I don't think it's going to happen tonight."

"Why not?" Jani clocks in and slips her green apron over her head. "Did he cancel?"

"No, it's me who cancelled. Or postponed."

"Why would you do that? Are you crazy? He was cute and totally into you."

"Fleur doesn't want me to go out tonight. If she wants me to stay with her, I will. No one will ever come before her."

"Does Ted know about Fleur?"

"Not yet." I couldn't figure out how to bring it up in a text. It's something I'd rather tell him in person or on the phone so I can gauge his response.

"Ooooh, that's smart. Most guys don't want baggage. I'd hook him first and then let him know." We open the door from the employee room and head out onto the floor. It's a good thing we have to open the store. It saves me from going off on Jani.

There are so many things wrong with her statement, but the sad truth is many people, both men and women, feel that way. If I start dating someone, he'll need to understand family.

I send a quick text to Ted, explaining that something came up and ask if he's free tomorrow. He quickly responds and says he was going to have to send me the same message.

I respond with a smiley-face emoji. A few minutes later, my phone dings again with Ted proposing plans for tomorrow night. See? This is going to work out just fine.

I don't think much about it, as the store is crowded this morning. September is the busy season in the crafting world—Halloween costumes, holiday craft fairs, and Christmas gifts mean we're usually hopping from store open to close. It helps to make the day pass quickly. I do love hearing about everyone's projects. There are a lot of creative people out there. I remember when I used to be one of them.

There appears to be a lull, which gives Morris, Jani, and me a chance to take quick breaks. We're supposed to get fifteen minutes but it's been so busy that we'll be lucky to get ten.

When my phone rings, I don't think twice about answering it, and don't look at the screen. Big mistake.

"Hello?"

"Kira! Thank you for answering. I was all prepared for it to go to voicemail."

I pull the phone away from my face to confirm what I suspect—fear. Yup, it's Tony.

"I didn't look to see who it was." I can't keep the displeasure out of my voice.

"I'm just glad you answered. I need to talk to you. Well, not need. I want to talk to you."

"You've got me." At least for the minute. "I'll give you a minute. I'm on a break at work, and I don't have much longer."

"I'm coming into town for work, and I was hoping to see you."

My mouth drops open. How could he?

He continues. "Nothing fancy. Unless you want fancy. But if you don't, I'm cool with that."

"Tony, I don't think that's a good idea."

"Are you busy tomorrow night?"

I can't help but smile. "Yes, in fact, I am. I have a date." And then, for some inexplicable reason, I go into detail—as much detail as I have—about Ted.

"So what are you guys going to do tomorrow?"

It's an odd question. He can only be asking because he's totally jealous. Totes jelly as Jani would say. Is it wrong that I sort of delight in telling him?

"Ted gets me, so he knows that I'm not a huge partier or anything, even though I do like me some karaoke. Anyway, we're gonna rent a movie, I think."

There's silence for a minute. Wow. I really got him.

"Kira, what exactly did this Ted guy say. How did he phrase your plans?"

"Why does it matter? We're going to rent a movie. That'll give us plenty of time to talk and get to know each other better."

"Where are you getting the movie from?"

"Why the Spanish Inquisition? Does it matter?"

Tony sighs. "How long have you been out of the dating scene?"

"Fifteen years. So what?"

"There's no more Blockbuster. Where are you getting the movie from?" He's all sorts of worked up. Dude, not cool.

"I think he said that he has Netflix. He wanted to just hang out and watch a movie."

"You mean Netflix and chill?"

Huh. That's exactly how Ted put it. "Yeah, so?"

"Do not go out with this guy."

Now it's my turn to sigh. I look at my watch. I've only got two more minutes. "Tony, it's a little late for this. You had your chance. You blew it."

"This isn't about me. This is about you."

"Tony, I've gotta get going." Jealousy is not an attractive trait.

Tony's voice rushes forth. "He thinks you're coming over to have sex!"

"What?"

"Netflix and chill. That's what it means. That you're going for a hookup. Which is fine if that's what you want, but you need to go in aware."

"Bye Tony." I disconnect.

That was so weird.

Tony must be smoking something. Ted's a nice guy and all he wants to do is hang out and watch a movie. I'm sure of it.

Chapter 13

"I'm so glad you could come over." Ted smiles a wide toothy grin. It's a little too toothy. It's probably not, but since my phone call yesterday, I can't stop thinking about Tony's sweet smile. I shake my head, trying to clear the thought.

I hand Ted the bottle of shiraz I've brought over. He looks at it and shrugs. "I don't drink wine. I don't even have a bottle opener."

"Um, okay. It was the thought I guess."

"I figured you were more of a beer girl. I picked up some of that." I follow Ted into his kitchen. His decor doesn't appear to be much removed from his frat boy days. He opens the fridge and pulls out a can.

Ugh. A can of beer? Really? Of course, he did meet me while I was belching, but I told him that was a total abnormality. I guess he didn't believe me. Ugh again. It's not only a can of beer, but crap beer too. I don't want to seem rude, so I take it.

I'm getting the sneaking suspicion that this date is not going to go how I planned. Not that I planned on much happening—I learned my lesson after the Tony debacle. I did shave my legs, but that's just because, well, you never do know.

The decor (and taste in beverages) does make me wonder how old Ted is. How can I bring that up without seeming weird? I run possible scenarios through my head. Turns out, I don't need to ask because the next words out of Rico Suavé's mouth are, "So, how old are you?"

I'm taken aback by his abruptness, probably because I was expending a tremendous amount of brainpower attempting to be stealth. "Um, ah, I'm thirty-five."

"I've been wondering about that. I'm twenty-nine. So, you're, like, a cougar."

I hardly think six years makes me a cougar, and he's the one who hit on me first, so it's not like I was pursuing him. Whatever. It doesn't matter. All that matters is two people enjoying each other's company.

"Um, okay. Did you want to get something to eat while we watch the movie? Pizza?"

"Oh. Um, I guess. Movie?"

"Yeah, weren't we going to watch a movie? What are you in the mood for? Comedy? Action? I'm a closet Marvel fan. Someday I'm going to hole up and watch them all in the correct order."

Ted looks at me like I've got three heads. "Oh, yeah, I don't like those movies. They're so unrealistic. I'm more into horror."

It's about now when I start to get an inkling that this may not be the date of my dreams. The signs had already been there, but I didn't want to see them. Now they're too obvious for me to ignore. Not that I'd had

Ted pegged for my soul mate, but I was hoping for someone who would be good company for a while.

We order a pizza and go out to the living room to pick a movie while we wait for it to arrive. I try not to notice that the couch is covered with a sheet and try even harder not to wonder what's underneath. If we hadn't already ordered the food, I'd probably come up with some excuse to cut this evening short. Maybe I'm not ready to date yet. Maybe it's Ted. Maybe it's because Tony called me yesterday and got in my head, and I can't stop thinking about what a disaster that night was. Maybe it's because this place gives me the heebie-jeebies.

The stilted conversation is interrupted by the delivery of the pizza. Thank goodness for the twenty-minutes-or-less guarantee. Maybe I can be home at a decent hour. I'm thinking about a dress I'd like to make for Fleur. I picked up the most adorable fabric the other day and have been thinking about what I want to do with it.

"Um, hello? Are you there?"

"Oh, sorry. What?"

"I didn't think you were listening."

"No, sorry. I must have spaced. I was thinking about a dress I'm going to make for my daughter."

"What? Daughter?"

Ooops. I forgot that I wasn't going to say anything about that for a while. Oh well, cat's out of the bag.

"Yes, she's five."

"Oh, like a real kid and everything." He shrugs. "I'm not a kid person, but I guess that's cool."

I don't know how young single men are supposed to react. Maybe "I guess that's cool" is the best I can hope for. I mean, it is a big deal. When you're first getting to know someone, it could be a lot of responsibility. I wonder if that's what he's thinking about, the impact he could have on Fleur's life. I mean, technically no one will replace her father, but if he doesn't show up again soon, she's not even going to remember him when she's older.

I continue eating my pizza, somewhat thankful for the awkward silence. It's certainly not romantic. It's ... blah. Ted is blah. He doesn't have much of a personality. And what personality he does have is giving me all the wrong vibes.

"You know, Fleur wasn't feeling that great earlier. I'd better call in to check on her. She was sick yesterday. It's why I had to cancel last night."

"Eeew. Are you contagious?"

Since it's made up illness, I don't know why I feel the need to provide reassurances "Oh, no. She's got a chronic lung illness. She coughs a lot and that sort of thing, but it's not catching. There can be a lot of phlegm." I have no idea why I'm saying this. Almost like I'm trying to repel him.

"That's gross. Are you done?" He nods toward my plate.

Oh, I'm done.

"Yeah, I guess." He clears my plate and quickly returns to the living room. "So ... you ready?"

"For what?" I have no idea what he's talking about.

"Out here or in my room?"

Oh. He must be talking about watching the movie. "Um, out here I guess." I'm thinking that I don't want to lead him on by going into his room. I can only imagine how ugly things could get in there.

Ted plops down on the couch next to me. "So, I gotta ask, what's the deal with the hair?"

"My hair?"

"Uh, yeah. What's the deal?"

"Um, I like something different. My natural color is brown. It's a little boring. I saw a girl once with bright pink hair, and I thought it was awesome. I've done tons of colors. It's quirky, like me."

"Quirky? Like, kinky?"

"No, quirky. I like things that are a little outside the mainstream or expected."

"That's what I was hoping for."

And before I can say anything else, Ted's on top of me, and his hands are definitely in places where my bathing suit covers.

The nice thing about being a solidly built woman is that I don't have to take that crap. I shove him off me, probably a little harder than I need to, and he lands with a *whomp* on the floor.

"What the hell?" Oooooh, he's pissed.

"Seriously? You're going to ask me that? What do you think you're doing?" I stand up and start to march to the kitchen to find my purse.

"Getting down to business. What else? You said you were chill."

That stops me in my tracks. Slowly, I turn back toward him.

"I didn't give you permission to touch me."

"Yeah you did. I asked where you wanted to do it and you said on the couch. What did you think I was talking about?"

There's no way on the face of this earth that I'm about to admit that I really thought we were going to watch a movie. "Yeah, well, I didn't. I'm out of here."

"You know, I thought you'd be thankful for someone like me giving attention to someone like you. The least you could do is give me a little."

I don't wait for him to finish that awful statement as I bolt out the door.

I make it almost all the way home before the tears start. Hot and heavy, they blur my vision, necessitating my pulling over so I don't wreck my car or kill someone. That would be all I need.

My phone dings. Ted has some nerve calling me right—

Are you kidding me? Tony? Why? Why is this happening to me?

Without thinking I answer. "What? What do you want? Why are you doing this to me?"

"Kira? Are you okay?"

"DO I SOUND OKAY?" I *may* be a tad bit on the edgy side at the moment.

"No, as a matter of fact, you don't. It's why I'm asking."

"No, the question should be why are you calling me? I thought I made it clear that I didn't want to talk to you, and even if I did, which I don't, I told you I had a date tonight."

"Yeah, well, I was worried about you and your date. I thought if the date wasn't going well, if I called you, you could use it as an excuse to get out of there. If it was going well, I figured you wouldn't answer."

I want to bang my head on the steering wheel. "So you're trying to be the good guy here."

He's quiet for a minute. Finally, in a low voice, barely audible, he says, "I thought I was a good guy. I just made a mistake."

I sniffle a bit. More than a bit. I could really use a tissue. "You were right. I hate to say it, but you were right."

"About?"

My sigh is long and loud. "Netflix and chill."

"That's what I was afraid of."

"For the record, I'm not chill."

"I'm not passing judgment if you are. But I thought you should know what you were getting into before you got there."

"Yeah, no. Even with your warning, I was still ambushed. Lucky for me I have brute strength. It goes along with being a chubby girl."

"You're not chubby."

"I ain't no waif either."

"No, you're a beautiful woman."

"Who tossed a guy across the room." It was to the floor, but what he doesn't know won't kill him.

"Atta girl."

I take a deep breath. "At least you got me to stop crying, so thanks."

"Mission accomplished. I'm just sorry I didn't call you earlier."

"Me too. It was a bad date, even before he accosted me."

"It's not that late. I'm still in town. Do you wanna hang out?"

"You mean Netflix and chill?"

"I'm not that kind of guy. I'm offended that you think so."

"I know for a fact you are. But I'm beat. Tonight took a lot out of me. When are you here until?"

I don't know why I asked this. What am I doing? I plead temporary insanity caused by cheap beer and a bad date.

"Tuesday, why?"

"Maybe we can do something tomorrow." WHAT AM I DOING?

I can practically hear the smile in his voice. "Sounds great. Text me when you get a chance."

I say goodbye and end the call. I am an idiot. What am I thinking?

Chapter 14

"Mom, I can't do this."

"Of course you can. Now pick up the phone, and text that young man."

"Young is the operative word. Mom, he's like a decade younger than I am. Plus, I'm not ready."

"You need to get out there." Mom's fluttering about the kitchen, cleaning up after breakfast. On Sundays, she usually makes something big. Today it was cinnamon praline Belgian waffles. Idiot me, I made the mistake of not only telling her about my disastrous date, but about Tony and how I may have accidentally sort of invited him to do something today.

"You never did," I say. It's not accusatory, simply fact.

"No, I never did. I couldn't. It was such a bad time. And I had to focus on you. By the time I realized you were okay, I'd been by myself for too long. I didn't want to have to deal with it again."

"Maybe that's what I should do. Focus on Fleur for a while. Stay out of the game. I'm fine with it. You know, I really need to process and reevaluate. It's too soon."

"Don't wait too long. You're still young. You still have more time."

"Time? For what?"

"More babies."

"Um, no thank you. I'm good with Fleur. I can't imagine starting over. And I don't want to." I peek out into the living room where she's coloring on the coffee table. She loves drawing and coloring, and really anything art related. I could watch her do it for hours. Last night taught me some valuable lessons. First, I need to brush up on the lingo. I'm not going to fall for something like that again. Second, I need to trust my gut. If I get a bad impression, I'm out of there. Third, but most important, I need to make sure Fleur is as important to him as she is to me.

I think that's going to be the largest stumbling block.

And it's okay. I can be like my mom. Sure I'm probably going to get lonely. It'll be fine. I can get a cat. Or two.

I'm making plans to become a crazy cat lady. This can't be a good sign.

I clear my dishes and go sit next to Fleur in the living room. She's drawing dresses. Oh my heart.

I love her so much, and I can't figure out how Stan could stay away for so long.

Then, as if I've summoned a beast from the underworld, my phone buzzes. It's him.

I don't want to answer. I've nothing to say to him. But I know I need to answer for my daughter.

"Yeah." I have to answer. I don't have to be nice.

"I want to see Fleur." I can already tell by his tone that this isn't going to be pleasant. I get up off the floor, managing not to grunt (go me!) and walk back to my bedroom. Fleur's too perceptive for her own good and doesn't need to be hearing this.

"I haven't been keeping you from seeing her."

"Well, I'm in town. I want to see her."

"You know where we are."

"Can you bring her to me? I want to introduce her to Bambi."

"Is that playing somewhere? I don't know if she's ready for it. She might get really upset when Bambi's mother dies."

"What the heck are you talking about? I want her to meet Bambi. My fiancée."

That's too much for me to process. He's engaged. Already. It's not even five flippin' months since he left me. And he's *engaged*? To someone named Bambi? I have no words. A mental image of my daughter's future step-mother floods my brain. It, of course, includes peroxide-blonde hair, collagen-filled lips, and silicone-filled breasts.

I can't believe Stan would go for that. Not the Stan I know.

But let's face it, it's not like I really know Stan. Obviously.

"Are you sure?"

"Sure about what?"

"Sure about having Fleur meet Ba ... Bambi." I stumble over the name. I don't know how I'm supposed to take her seriously. "She's not even used to the idea that we're split up yet. This could be very upsetting to her."

"What have you been telling her? You didn't tell her I was coming back? Bambi said you'd try to use Fleur to reel me back in."

This is where I have the maturity that a twenty-something lacks. "Stan, I know this will come as a bruise to your ego, but I don't want you back. What you did—that was one of my deal-breakers."

He doesn't respond for a minute. He knows what it means. I can be pretty laid-back and forgiving, except when it comes for my hard lines. He crossed that line. Plus, not that I'm going to say this to him, but why would I want someone who doesn't want me?

"Well, we're getting married, so Fleur needs to meet her step-mother."

Even though, logically, I knew that would happen, the words hit me like a punch in the gut. I sink onto the bed, my legs no longer able to support me.

I need to say something, so I take a deep breath and begin. "You've been away for a while. Fleur keeps questioning if you're coming back and why you don't want to see her. She's been struggling. This is not going to be easy for her."

"You mean it won't be easy for you."

"Stan, why do you keep putting this back on me? I'm not the one who did this. I didn't fight you on it. I signed the papers. I've taken on all responsibility for our daughter—"

"I pay support."

I want to punch him. Can someone invent an app so you can punch someone through the phone? "Right. You do. But that's not the day-to-day. Every day. All day. I think I know what she needs, and she's going to need time with this. I think you need to take her by yourself first and talk to her about your future plans."

"I was hoping you'd tell her."

Oh hell no.

"Absolutely not. This is your mess. It's not my circus, not my monkeys. I'm not touching this one."

He's quiet for a minute. "So, how do you think I should tell her?" His voice has changed, and instead of being argumentative, it's introspective. It's the old Stan. I don't want to give him any answers. I want him to have to work for it, but since it's dealing with our daughter's heart, I need to put my feelings aside.

Crap, when did I get to be so mature?

"First and foremost and always, you need to reassure her that you still love her and that nothing, and I mean *nothing*, will ever change that."

"Obviously I love her."

"She doesn't think so."

"Jeez Kira, what have you been telling her? I'm not paying for therapy when you screw her all up." His voice is hard again. The new Stan. I wonder where this person came from. It's not the man I married. This is a man I want to punch in the wiener.

"It's not what I've been telling her but what you've been showing her. You aren't here. I've stopped telling her when you're supposed to come, because I can't bear to add to her heartbreak when you end up cancelling. You've broken her heart. You may think that you just left me, but you really left her too. She feels deserted."

"This is certainly a mess."

"Yes Stan, it is. It's your mess. You did this."

"How is this my fault?"

Oh my God. I don't know this man anymore. I don't know how to talk to him, and there's certainly no reasoning with him. He really is totally dense.

"Stan, you asked my opinion and I gave it to you. Don't be a jerk about it. Own what you've done."

"I'm just trying to be happy."

It's another punch in the gut. The implication that I—that we—didn't make him happy. That's the hardest part, because I thought we were happy. I know I was.

"I know you are, and you've made it clear where your priorities lay. I don't think you should introduce your *fiancée* yet, especially considering how little you've wanted to do with Fleur. Why even bother?" Getting that word out will never be easy.

"Whatever. We'll pick her up at one."

I disconnect without responding. I don't know what happened to Stan. I only know the change has not been for the good. I look at the clock. It's almost eleven. I've got about two hours to figure out how to prevent my daughter's life from being destroyed.

No sweat.

Chapter 15

He at least had the decency to leave Bambi in the car when he came to the door. My mom had the good sense to guard the knives and put the throwing stars away. Okay, she doesn't have throwing stars. At least I don't think she has them. I sort of wish she did.

A glance into the front seat of his F-150 reveals that my mental picture was pretty much spot on. It makes me want to vomit.

Not just want to vomit apparently. As soon as I kiss Fleur goodbye, I run to the bathroom and relieve my stomach of its contents. And then I cry. A good hot cry that mourns for my daughter and the innocence she's about to lose. For my partnership that apparently meant so much more to me than it did to my partner. For my life which is not what I thought it would be. And for my sanity, which apparently has temporarily left me as I pull out my phone and call Tony.

"Kira? Are you okay? You sound sick."

"No, I've been crying. Again." God, I'm so sick of crying.

"What's wrong? Don't waste energy on that loser from last night."

"No, it's my ex-husband. He just picked up Fleur. He hasn't seen her in a long time, and he's going to introduce her to his fiancée. *Bambi.*"

"Bambi? Is that her stripper name?"

I have to laugh, because that was my thought too. "Probably. She certainly looks like it."

"I'm getting a mental image."

"If it contains silicone, collagen, and way too much makeup, then you've got it."

"That's what I was picturing."

I sigh. "I can't believe he replaced me with that."

"He's stupid."

"No, he's not."

"Yes, he must be. I'm fairly certain that *Bambi* isn't half the woman you are."

"I'm guessing she's about half the woman I am. At least size-wise."

"Oh. I hadn't pictured her as a little person."

While it's totally not what I meant, it still makes me laugh and strokes my ego that he doesn't follow up with one of the lame things you hear like, "You're big boned."

Then I remember why I was so upset. "Fleur didn't even know that he was dating someone. This is only the third time she's seen Stan since he left in April. She's having major abandonment issues. I don't blame her."

"I don't get how guys can do that to their kids. I can't imagine my dad ever leaving and not coming back."

"Yeah, well I can. My dad did it. I think I thought that even though Stan reminded me of him, Stan was a more refined, improved version."

"Oh, I'm sorry about your dad. I didn't know."

"How could you? We've never talked about this sort of thing. Let's face it, all I know about your family came from Michele."

"Kira?"

"Yeah." I'm finally off the bathroom floor and have washed my face. My roots are growing in again and my teal is fading. I need to think about what hair color I'm going to do next.

"Do you want to go grab a bite to eat or go for a walk or something? My hotel is very boring and I'd like to see a little of the area. I could use an experienced tour guide."

Why the hell not? What have I got to lose? Plus, it's not like anything's going to happen with Tony and me. That ship sailed a long time ago.

"You know, that sounds like a good idea. I could really use a friend right now."

We exchange the details. He's in a hotel in downtown Columbus, in the Arena District. There are plenty of shops and places to eat, plus a great park nearby where we can walk around. I relay this information to him.

"Okay, whatever you say. You're the boss."

"And don't you forget it."

Once we disconnect, I wash my face again. I quickly French braid my hair, loving how the colors overlap and intertwine as the plait travels down my back. My hair is getting a little cumbersome—it's almost to my waist. I may think about a new style, something shorter, the next time I go to see Emay.

I put on a pair of well-worn, comfortable jeans. You can tell fall is slowly seeping in, despite the bright sun and warm temperatures today. I wear a tank top and layer a flannel shirt over it.

Then I take it off. It looks like I'm trying too hard to be a hipster. Then I try a sundress, but it looks ridiculous with my hair. I think I was in the red-orange phase when I bought this dress. Back to jeans and a baseball-jersey-style T-shirt. Casual. Not too dated. I don't think I look like a soccer mom, but I don't look like I'm trying too hard to be young either.

Why am I even trying? This isn't a date. This is soooo not a date. No, this is just friends hanging out.

If it were a date, I'd wear perfume. I don't need that. Well, maybe I'd better put on some Bath and Body Works body spray. There. I smell like lavender and honey, but it's not perfume. It's not like effort. Not date effort.

I head into town on I-70. Traffic's light on a Sunday afternoon, and I get there earlier than I'd expected. If this were a date, I'd wait until the agreed-upon time, or even a few minutes past. Since it's not, I park and send a text telling Tony that I'd made good time.

He's dressed casually as well in jeans and a T-shirt. He's got that clean-cut, J. Crew model kind of look. There's a tinge of hipster in the cut of his clothing, but it's subtle. I don't think he'll be sporting a man-bun anytime soon.

I pull my sunglasses down to shade against the bright sun. There are a lot of gray days in Ohio, so the crisp blue sky is a treat that I always appreciate. We start out heading toward Short North. Most of the art galleries are closed on a Sunday afternoon, but there are plenty of interesting windows to gaze upon.

"Why are you here again? What is it you do?" I don't know that it's ever come up before, and I feel like I should know, but it escapes me in the moment.

"Insurance. I'm an actuary for Nationwide."

"Isn't that one of the most boring jobs ever? I remember someone talking about it, saying that it's incredible money, but it's, like, super boring."

"It can be, but I like numbers."

"I am not a numbers person. No math, no thank you. I don't know what I'm going to do when I have to help Fleur with her homework."

"You can call me. I seriously like numbers."

"But didn't you say your job was soul sucking?"

"Well, the whole corporate aspect. And even though I like numbers, it can get a little tedious. What about you? Aren't you a designer?"

"Yeah, I went to Columbus School of Design."

"You know, there's tons of math in sewing. In fact, it's impressive how quickly you sewing people do math in your heads to calculate fabric and seams and all that stuff."

I think about it for a minute. "I'm not like pencil and paper, quadratic equations math."

Tony laughs, kicking a stone in his way. "You know what a quadratic equation is, so I'd say that's a start."

"I didn't say I know what it is. I know of it. That's about it. I remember my brother bellyaching about them."

"Oh, I didn't know you had a brother. Does he live around here?"

Now it's my turn to kick a stone or two. We turn down a side street and approach Goodale Park. I head toward the pond, not really waiting to see if Tony's keeping up.

I find a bench and sit down. There are mallard ducks and Canada geese everywhere. A turtle pokes his head out of the water for a brief second. Once Tony sits down, I continue. "My brother died right after he graduated from high school. He had hemophilia. He was horsing around with friends, tripped and hit his head. They couldn't stop the bleeding."

"Oh, Kira, I'm so sorry. I had no idea. I ..."

"No, it's fine. It was a long time ago. He wanted to live life like every normal kid. He didn't want to be in a plastic bubble. I wish he'd been a little more careful. He would have been able to do more."

"I can see both sides."

"I can too, especially now that I'm a mom. I still don't know how my mom dealt with it. But she did. My dad, on the other hand, did not."

"You don't seem to want to talk about him much."

"He took off not long after Jimmy died. Couldn't handle it. I know he blamed my mother for Jimmy being sick in the first place, which is kind of crappy."

"Why would it be your mother's fault?"

I'm not a science person, but this I do know the answer to. I've had to explain it a lot. It took Stan a while to grasp. "You know how boys have XY chromosomes and girls are XX, and the X comes from the mother and the dad gives the other one, either an X or a Y, and that determines the gender?"

Tony nods. "Yup, I think. Tenth grade bio is starting to flash in front of my eyes."

"Basically. So, with hemophilia, the mother's X chromosome is defective in about fifty percent of her eggs. With Jimmy, the X she provided was defective. Since the other chromosome is a Y, the disease is allowed to express itself, even though it's recessive, because there's not another X to dominate it."

"I didn't realize I was going to get a science lesson. I would have studied or something."

I give him a playful slap. "So my dad blamed my mom for her defective X, but it was his fault for providing a Y. They were both to blame."

"Okay, I can see that. No one's fault, just one of those things."

"My mom's brother had it too. Most of the males in her family did. But there's a fifty percent chance that they won't have it, so people keep rolling the dice."

Tony frowns. "What about you?"

"Girls don't get hemophilia, since the X from Dad is dominant and doesn't let the defective X win. But, they can carry that defective gene and keep passing it down, which is what happened to my mom." I pause. "I'm lucky. I don't have it. I'm not a carrier. Fleur is not a carrier. I can't pass it on. I got off scot-free."

"That's certainly good news."

"Yes and no. Survivor's guilt and all."

"I can see that. It's family. I'm from a big Italian family. They're going to guilt you about one thing or another."

"True dat."

Tony looks at me. "I'm glad you called."

His eyes draw me in. "I'm glad I called too."

Good thing this is not a date. Otherwise, I'd be in big trouble.

Chapter 16

"How'd it go?" Mom practically pounces on me the moment I walk through the door.

"Fine." It's hard to keep the smile off my face. It's been a long time since I was this relaxed.

"Fine? That's all you're going to give me is 'fine?' I sit with you through all the crying and all I get is 'fine?'"

"Okay, it was good."

Mom drops her dishtowel in an overly dramatic fashion. "You are going to give me gray hair." For the record, I've heard this line my whole life. She started going gray when she was twenty, long before I made an appearance. I don't remember her with anything but silver hair.

"Too late for that." I smile at her. "No, it was good. He's nice, but we're just friends. That's all I want right now." I neglect to tell her about the hook-up that wasn't when I was in Montabago. She may be my best friend, but there are some things you don't want to share with your mom. "Plus, he's young. Too young for me."

"How old is he?"

"Um, I think about twenty-five. So, way too young. I could have babysat for him."

"Where does he live again?"

"He's from Upstate New York but lives in the city now. He's Michele's cousin. She's dating his roommate, Lincoln."

"Oh, so is she doing the younger man thing?"

"Sort of, but Michele's younger than I am. She turned thirty while we were on the show. Well, while she was on it. I'd already been eliminated. It's not that bad for her."

"It might be fun to be a cougar."

Mom's words remind me of that creep Ted, causing a shudder to run through my body.

"No, thanks. I'll pass. And if I want to date, I'll find someone my own age. I think that'll be for the best."

"Are you sure?"

"It's not like he even lives around here. I mean, how would that even work? I can't do the long-distance thing. And it's not like I'm going to fly to New York one weekend a month. What's the point? I don't even know if I want to have another relationship at this time. But I do know that if I were going to pursue something, it would be with someone who had potential for longevity. I don't want to waste any more time on mistakes." As I give my monologue, I unload the dishwasher. Mom's making German potato salad and is creating a new pile of dishes.

"Wow, that's so mature. And unromantic."

"You're one to talk, you know."

She stills, which makes me feel badly about insulting her. I don't mean to hurt her feelings.

"I had my reasons."

"So do I. I don't have the energy to waste on someone who doesn't deserve it."

"And this Tony person doesn't deserve it?"

"Yeah. I mean no. I mean, it's not right. If he were ten years older and lived here, maybe I'd consider thinking about it. But those two obstacles are simply too big to overcome."

"Are they?"

"Um, yeah. He's too young. We're at different points in our lives. We always will be." I put the last dish away and close the dishwasher. I turn toward Mom. "I did tell him about Jimmy and Dad though."

She gives me her tight, sad smile. "You don't talk about that a lot."

"I don't talk about that ever."

"So why did you tell him then?"

I shrug. "I dunno. It sort of came out. Before I knew it, I was giving him a genetics lesson in X-linked recessive genes."

"And he still said he'd talk to you again?"

"Thanks for the vote of confidence, Mom." I know she's kidding, but my ego's a little on the fragile side.

"Is he still in town?" She's adding the bacon to the pan. It's my favorite part. I snatch a little piece and pop it in my mouth.

"Yeah, until at least Wednesday, I think."

"I made way too much salad for the two of us. Why don't you call him and see if he wants to come over for dinner?"

"I can't do that." What could she be thinking? I know things have changed since I was dating in the last century, but I'm pretty sure you can't call a guy twice in the same day. I tell her as much.

"I didn't think you were interested in dating him."

"I ... um ... I'm not, but it's still not done. It's not cool."

"You're not cool." Her voice is light and teasing.

"Of course I'm cool. I have blue hair."

"That's not cool. That's ridiculous. Now call that young man."

"Young being the operative word," I mutter as I head to my room. While I appreciate the support and the company my mom provides, sometimes I feel like I've reverted back to being a teenager. Though, ironically, when I was a teenager, I was the one providing support and company for my mom.

Despite my better judgment, I text Tony and invite him for dinner. I hope I don't come off as desperate and lonely. I know I totally am, but I don't want him to think that.

Tony responds immediately. He's in. I text him the directions and take the next few minutes to ponder what I've done.

I must be losing my mind. It's the only logical explanation. I text Michele about the latest developments.

The return text is full of emojis and squeals. Or what I imagine are squeals. More like a bunch of capital letters strung together. Then she sends an odd text.

Tora!

I text back. *What does the Jewish bible have to do with it?*

Tony + Kira = Tora

I am too old for this. I text her as much. She responds with *Kiny?*

I can only imagine that Kiny is Kira + Tony. Either way, neither works. Like Tony and me. Makes no sense. I shouldn't have said anything to Michele. She still doesn't know what happened in Montabago. I'm never speaking of that again.

Do I change? No. Changing would seem like I'm interested. I should at least brush my hair and teeth. Maybe touch up my makeup a little.

As I'm finishing, the doorbell rings. That was quick.

I cannot let Mom get the door. Lord only knows what she would do or say if I'm not right there to censor her. I hear her voice. Oh crap, I'm too late.

It will be fine. I'm thirty-five. My mother can't embarrass me anymore.

Oh but she can. I didn't exactly pay attention to what my mom was wearing earlier. She's always had a more ... eclectic ... fashion sense. Today is no different. Her top is fine, a nondescript, striped mom-shirt. It's the pants that give me pause as I walk up behind her. They're jeans. Mom jeans, but that's not the issue. Oh no. It's the fact that for some inexplicable reason, she's sewn a patch on the back pocket. Staring back at me is a yellow, have-a-nice-day happy face. On her butt.

There is nothing in any of my fashion training that could or would justify this.

Maybe she won't turn around. Maybe he won't see.

"Come on in. Follow me."

I close my eyes and wish this embarrassment away. Upon opening, I see that it's another failed wish. And of course, Tony's looking at her posterior. How can he not with the big yellow beacon calling his attention?

He tears his eyes away and meets my gaze. I can see the laughter in them. I shake my head in response.

He laughs. "You can dress them up but you can't take them out."

"More like you can take them out but you can't dress them up."

"What are you two talking about?"

"Nothing, Mom."

"Oh, I forgot, I'm meeting Madge for dinner. You two will have to manage on your own. Everything's on the table." And with that, she rushes by and is out the door.

"That was subtle."

"Not even close. Obvious is her middle name though." I gesture for Tony to sit down at the kitchen table while I set about putting the food out. Mom outdid herself. In addition to the German potato salad, there are bratwurst and sauerkraut, cucumber salad, and baked beans.

"She seems fun."

"I think I'll keep her, at least for now." I sit down to Tony's left. "I'm not sure what I would've done through all this without her support. She helps me out tons with Fleur."

"That's probably a good thing, right?"

"Obviously. I don't know how I'd work or do anything. I know people can be single parents—I am one now, and so is my mom—but I never planned on being a single parent. I'm figuring it out, but until now, I never even thought about it."

"It's gotta be tough."

"Yeah, not quite what I'd planned for, but I'm rolling with it. I don't have much other choice now do I?"

"Do you want your husband back?"

"No." My answer is quick and automatic.

"Really?" Tony's giving me a skeptical look.

"Really. What he did is unforgivable. I don't tolerate cheating. Plus, there's no way I could possibly respect someone who has such little respect for me."

"That's a mature way to look at it."

His comment reminds me of our impressive age gap. If I'd even been considering something between us—which I'm totally not—this serves as a reminder of why it wouldn't work.

"You have a way with words. Every woman loves to be referred to as mature." My voice is light. I'm not hurt, but it's certainly not the most flattering thing I've ever heard. On the other hand, it's not the worst thing he's said to me either.

"No, it's a good thing."

"Whatever you say, Martha Stewart." I shovel a large forkful of German potato salad into my mouth.

"What does Martha Stewart have to do with anything? Have you seen her show with Snoop Dogg?"

Another point about the generational divide. It's a chasm that's too large to overcome. Definitely.

Chapter 17

"Michele, I hate you. This is all your fault. I never want to talk to you again. Call me when you get a chance." I know the message makes no sense. Nothing makes sense anymore. I know how things should be.

Scratch that; I thought I knew how things should be. I don't know anything anymore.

I'm a single mother. And I never thought that could happen. Though I used to worry obsessively about a truck accident, I couldn't really imagine myself a widow. Never in a million years did I think I would be a divorced woman. My vows meant something—everything—to me.

I never thought I'd have the gumption to go on a TV show. Granted I didn't do well, but the experience was a once-in-a-lifetime thing. Then, getting to help make the winning designs and fly to Europe to assist at the royal wedding—never could have seen that coming either.

Maybe this is the trajectory my life is taking. I get it. Highs and lows. I appreciate the highs, but I don't have to like the lows, and I don't have to keep accepting unwanted lobs from out in left field.

Like Tony.

There is nothing about Tony that makes sense. He's too young. He lives over six hundred miles away. He's not looking for anything serious; certainly not the baggage of instantaneous family.

I've already told myself that Tony is not someone I should pursue.

There's a soft knock on the door. "Kira? Are you okay?"

I sigh. I guess I need to go back out there and face him. I don't want to. It's so much easier to talk myself out of being interested when I'm not looking at his cute smile or warm brown eyes.

"Yeah, I'm fine." I open the door. Yup, definitely easier when I can't see him.

"I was getting worried. You've been gone a while."

"No, I'm okay."

"Did I say something? I know I do that with you. Most of the time, I don't even know what I'm saying that's wrong, I just know that it is."

I smile. Adorable. Totally adorable. "No, you didn't say anything wrong. This time, it's me. All me."

"Do you want to talk about it in here?" he gestures toward my bed.

Oh, yes I do.

No, I don't. I can't. I shouldn't.

I could ...

No. I need to be strong.

"Yeah, why don't you have a seat to talk. *Just talk.*"

Tony holds his hands up in front of him. "I only want to talk. I know we're only friends. I'm okay with that."

That should make me happy. I should not have a sinking feeling in the pit of my stomach when he says that. I can handle friends. I cannot handle more. So, yeah, friends. I can do this.

"I was calling Michele to yell at her."

"Why do you want to yell at Michele?"

I can't tell him the real answer. I don't even know why I said that. "Um, because I haven't heard an update from her about how she and Lincoln are doing."

"And you thought of that now?"

"Well, yeah, I guess." I am so lame.

He's going to know how lame I am. I don't want him to know that. Wait—why is it even important to me?

It's not.

I lie. It is.

"I don't want to be friends," I blurt out before I can stop myself.

His face falls. I don't want to make his face fall. I don't want to be responsible for that. "It's okay." He stands up. "I should be going. I've got an early meeting anyway."

Tony heads out of my room, and I can't do anything but sit there and watch his fine behind leave. Why did I say that? Because I'm an idiot, that's why.

"Tony, wait!" I run after him, just in time to see him open the door to a stunned looking Stan.

In the future, I might plead temporary insanity in regard to my next actions. There's certainly no way I can sanely justify what I do. Grabbing Tony's arm, I spin him around to face me and plant one on him. A big one. I can feel from Tony's reaction that he's a bit stunned. I don't blame him. I'm stunned too.

He pulls back slightly and out of the corner of my eye I see Stan glare. Giving Tony my best mental telepathy, I implore him with my eyes to go along with it. Either he understands or he's a horn dog, because this time, Tony initiates the kiss. It's intense and deep, and for a minute, I really do forget that my scuzzball ex is watching us. When Tony kisses me, the whole world seems to melt away.

"Nice, Kira. You act like that with your daughter around? Maybe she should stay with me more." Stan does nothing to hide the disdain in his voice. His threat, even though I know he'd never go through with it, is enough to make me pull away from Tony.

"Oh, I didn't see you there. Tony was just leaving." I choose to ignore the hurt and confusion in Tony's eyes. I am a crappy human being. I know it. He probably should too. Save us both some hurt. I'm not ready for this. I'll call him after Stan leaves and apologize.

Tony gives me one last look, but I can't meet his eyes. With resignation, he drops his head and mumbles something as he passes Stan, who is standing with his chest puffed out. Ugh, seriously? Stan dropped me like I was on fire and now he wants to act all territorial? I don't think so.

I want to call after Tony, but I can't bring myself to.

"Who was that loser?"

"Nice, Stan." It's then I notice that Fleur isn't even out of the car. "Where's Fleur?"

"Oh, uh, she's still in the car. Bambi's trying to talk to her. She's upset."

"WHY? What did you do to her?"

"Um, uh, Fleur got all hysterical when Bambi told her she was going to be her new mom."

New mom?

"NEW MOM? ARE YOU KIDDING ME?"

"Dude, why are you yelling? You need to calm down."

Suddenly, I understand how murder is possible, although I'm pretty sure any female on the jury would call this justifiable homicide. The ape basically threatens to take my daughter away because I have a guy over, yet lets his bimbo say she's going to be her new mother. Not that I have much respect left for Stan after the way he's treated me, but any that might have remained has flown out the window. I want him out of my sight. If I never had to see him again, it will be too soon.

"Stan, bring Fleur in. I think Bambi should stay in the car. And then you need to leave. If you open up your trap and say one more moronic thing, I cannot be responsible for what I may do." In my head, I'm thinking about ways to remove his testicles.

With that, I turn and storm into the kitchen. There are so many emotions swirling through my head right now. I cannot believe Stan. I mean, if I had to guess, I'd say he was jealous of Tony. Which is stupid because he's the one who cheated on me—for two years. So why would he be jealous? I can't think of any other reason why he'd lash out so immediately and with such a threatening tone. He knows how to push my buttons, that's for sure.

I can't sit and stew, no matter how much I'd like to, because there's a little girl in tears running into my arms.

"It's okay, baby. I'm here. You're okay," I murmur into her hair, holding her close to me. How dare they do this to her? How can Stan hurt her like this? "You're okay, baby." I repeat my words, hoping they sink in and reassure her.

"Mommy, I thought you were gone again. She said she was going to be my mom."

"She's going to be your *stepmother*."

"What's that?"

Oh gosh, now that's a loaded question, because the first word I want to say is evil and talk about Cinderella and Snow White. I know that I can't—shouldn't—because someday I might want to introduce a stepfather to Fleur, and I won't want her to think bad things about him. I must do the adult thing, no matter how much I want to be childish and get revenge.

"I'm still going to be your mommy. I'll always be your mommy. It just means that she's going to be married to Daddy, and she's going to love you like you're her daughter." And as I say this, the bile begins to rise in my throat. What if this totally screws Fleur up? I need to figure out how to talk to Stan in a calm and rational way so we get this right.

"How can Daddy marry her when he's married to you? Are you going to be on *Sister Wives*?"

I should be astounded that my five-year-old knows about *Sister Wives*, but I also know that my mother is addicted to TLC and doesn't always use the best judgment if her "show" is on.

"No, we're not going to be on *Sister Wives*."

"Then how is Dad going to marry Bambi when he's married to you?"

Yeah, so maybe I've been a little passive in filling Fleur in on things. I mean, she's only five. How much does she need to know? Apparently more than I figured.

"Daddy and Mommy aren't married anymore. We're divorced."

"Divorced? *Divorced?*" She stands up straight, hands on her hips and gives me a look that's full of attitude.

I swear, sometimes Fleur sounds more like a fifteen-year-old than a five-year-old. I have a feeling I'm going to be in lots of trouble in about ten years.

"Yes, honey. Daddy and I aren't married anymore."

"Why not?"

Because your father's a lying, cheating louse. No, that's probably not the best answer. "Sometimes, people grow apart and don't love each other the same way anymore."

"Does that mean that we might grow apart?"

I'm going to need a second job just to afford all the therapy Fleur's going to need. "Oh, no. The way a mommy and daddy love their child is different from being married. We can never fall out of love with you."

"Then why did Daddy stop loving you?"

Now isn't that the ten-thousand-dollar question?

Chapter 18

"Tony, it's Kira. Again. Look, I just wanted to say again how sorry I am about everything. It's, well, I'm messing this all up. Again. And how many times can I say again in one message? Before I say it again, I'd better hang up. Again, I'm sorry. Ugggggh."

I am so smooth. This is the second time I've called him in two days. I think I officially qualify as a loser at this point. It's probably a good thing I'm giving up on dating. Well, dating Tony, that is. Obviously our stars are not aligned. It's not meant to be. I'm not going to force it. It shouldn't be this hard. Marriage wasn't this hard.

On the other hand, maybe if we'd worked a little harder, Stan and I would still be married. Truth be told, I still have no idea what happened between us. Why he strayed. Why he thought someone else would be better to come home to each night than his wife and daughter.

It's me. That's the only logical answer. I wasn't enough for him. Or, more likely, I was too much woman for him. It's not that I'm huge, but no one's going to mistake me for a waif. And then there's the hair. Stan was the one who encouraged me to do it in the first place, right after I graduated college. He was getting another tattoo, and since I wouldn't, we came up with this small act of rebellion. Except I really liked it—and I thought he did too. Maybe it's sad now that I'm in my mid-thirties and pudgy and drive a sensible, safe, sedan.

Maybe I got boring. I'm much less of a night owl than I used to be. I mean, who isn't at my age? I have to get up early with Fleur. She's up by about six-thirty every day, whether she needs to be or not. It doesn't matter what time I go to bed, I'm still getting woken up at six-thirty. So I've adjusted. I rarely make it through the ten o'clock shows anymore. I do sensible things like DVR shows that I want to watch, schedule regular doctor appointments, and try to eat vegetables at every meal.

Oh, God, I got boring.

Even my brightly colored hair has not been enough to keep me from being boring. Well, no wonder Stan left. I'd have left me too if something better came along.

I guess being on a TV show wasn't interesting enough. Probably because he was already out the door—I gave him the opportunity to leave with the least amount of hassle. How could I not have known? How did I not see that he was distant?

Because he was always distant.

Oh crap, does that mean our whole relationship was a lie? When we first got together, I always wondered what Stan saw in me. An awkward design student—somewhat chic yet so not. I was a hipster before hipsters existed. Now that I'm older, I just look like I'm trying too hard.

Stan had been a scrawny high school student. After high school, he went to work in physical jobs which started the beefing up process. I've only ever known the bulky Stan who looks like he could tear down a sixty-foot tree with his bare hands. I've lost count of his tattoos. So many of them blend together that I don't even know if we could tally them up at this point. I shudder to think about the amount of money he's spent on them in the past fifteen years. In fact, the day we met was the day he'd gone for his first tattoo—a tribal band around his right bicep. Clichéd, but so late 1990s. If I had a tattoo myself, it would have been a tramp stamp. Thank goodness I didn't do that.

Better this thing with Tony hasn't gone anywhere. If I wasn't interesting enough to keep Stan, there's no way I could keep someone like Tony for long. And, let's face it, I'm in no hurry to do this whole rejection thing again. Frankly, it sucks.

This is what I tell Jani when I return to the fabric counter after break. "I'm done dating. I can't do this. I can't do it to me. I can't do it to Fleur."

"So you're never going to have sex again?" Of course that's where Jani's mind goes. She's got a libido I didn't know could exist in a woman. Either that or she's the world's biggest liar. In all honesty, sex is pretty much the furthest thing from my mind. The thought of opening myself up in that way, at this point, is difficult to process.

"Not in the foreseeable future, it would seem. I guess I blew my chances when I was in Europe." And I know it's true. All those months ago, the idea of a meaningless fling seemed like a fun thing to do. Now, all I can see is hurt and distrust. There's no way that I can put myself out there again.

It's a good thing I've been such a colossal disaster when it comes to Tony. If you look at him and then look at me, it's obvious there's no way it would have ever worked out. Undoubtedly he'd find himself a young chippy—someone worthy of him. Someone that I'm not.

"Well, I guess I shouldn't have signed you up for online dating then."

I drop the bolt of calico that I'm pricing. "You did what?"

Jani won't make eye contact. Probably a good thing, because if she looked me square in the eye, I'd probably punch her right about now. "Can I help you?" She attempts to help a white-haired lady who's obviously browsing and doesn't need any help.

"Jani, what did you do? You shut it down right now. I am not doing that internet dating. Just because my husband has moved on, it doesn't mean I want that sort of thing. Why can't everyone accept that I'm fine the way I am?"

She gives me a pointed look. "Are you really fine?"

I know that the answer is no, but I also know it should be okay for my answer to be no. My life has been blown apart. I've gone through some depressive-type episodes. I'm struggling to find a new life while at the same time keeping things as stable for my daughter as possible. It totally sucks.

"I will be, if you let me be. Things will happen in their own time."

I only wish I believed it. One of my biggest fears at this moment is that I'm going to end up alone like my mom. Sure, she seems happy, but I've often wondered throughout the years how much of it was an act—a front she put on so I didn't know. Just like I'm doing with Fleur.

I've finally picked up the fabric I dropped and have refolded it. "Jani, I know you mean well. I'm just not ready. I wouldn't know how to swipe up or down or whatever."

I hear a small chuckle from behind me. "I think you mean right or left."

I turn to see a man, probably about my age, who looks somewhat familiar. I can't place where I might know him from though. "Whatever. You know what I mean. I'm too old for all that newfangled technology."

"Really? You seem like the hip mom in class."

Hip mom in class? Who is this joker?

While those are my inner thoughts, they must be plastered across my face. He extends his hand. "Ross Stevens. Zoe's dad."

Zoe ... Zoe ... "Oh, Zoe! Fleur was talking about her the other day." Yes, of course. Now if only I could remember what Fleur was saying. I sort of get the feeling that it wasn't super positive, but that could be my memory playing tricks on me. It does that.

"Zoe just loves Fleur. Talks about her nonstop."

Now I feel like the world's crappiest mother. Fleur's only been in kindergarten for a few weeks now, and I don't even know who her friends are. I went to the opening day festivities and of course to the open house, but other than that, I haven't had a tremendous amount to do with the new school. I make sure Fleur has her sneakers on gym day and that her snack is peanut free, but truth be told, I've been phoning it in. Wow, I suck. Maybe if I concentrated less on me, Stan, and the whole Tony debacle, I'd be a better mother.

"That's so cute. Listen, we should get the girls together for a play date this weekend."

"That sounds great. Zoe has piano, dance, and soccer on Saturday, but she's free after one."

"That sounds like a busy morning." Huh. Maybe I need to enroll Fleur in more things. She does dance, but it's only one day a week. What else are five-year-olds supposed to do? Gosh, I am failing so hard at momming right now.

"So will one work?"

"Sure. Wait, no, I have to work until four. How about five? I'll cook dinner."

"Awesome. I know Zoe will be so excited. Oh, and FYI, she's gluten and dairy free."

"So pizza is out, then?" I have no experience with food restrictions like this. Where have I been the past five years?

Ross looks at me for a minute. Apparently my humor is lost on him. "This is serious. Maybe we shouldn't do a meal together yet."

"Oh, I'm sorry. I was trying to be funny. I'll do fruits and veggies and um ... what else?"

He gives me the name of an organic, gluten-free chicken nugget that I'm pretty sure is going to cost more than a whole chicken. Maybe Zoe isn't the best friend to pick—I can see this getting costly.

We swap numbers, and then I cut his fabric for him. Apparently, he's in set design at a local theater and is working on a new production.

"Okay, well I'll see you on Saturday then!" I'm a little too cheerful, too forced. I can hear it. I hope he can't.

"It's a date!" he calls as he heads toward the front of the store. I can see Morris watching the whole thing, and know I'm going to be pressed for an explanation.

Once Ross is out of earshot, Jani lets out a low whistle. "Dang, girl, you work fast. You don't have to worry about swiping left or right. Your milkshake is bringing all the boys to the yard."

I have no idea what she means by that, but at least this will get her off my back with the online dating thing.

Not that this is a date. Because I'm not dating. End of story.

Chapter 19

"So, like, do you have lots of tattoos? You keep them hidden well. Trying not to give the other moms more to talk about?"

Ross' question catches me off guard. It's fairly random, considering he and Zoe have only been in my house for about four minutes. The girls immediately disappeared back into Fleur's room, leaving Ross and me standing awkwardly in the front hall. I've finally remembered my manners and ushered him into the kitchen for a hot beverage. We've not gone beyond what to drink, so this question drops on me like a bomb.

"Ah, um, what?"

"You know, your tattoos? How many do you have? Do you purposefully keep them hidden so people won't talk about you?"

Okay, this is messed up. "Um, no. I don't."

"Oh, right. Okay. Maybe the days I've seen you, you just happened to be fully covered."

"No, it's not that I cover them up. I don't have any."

"Really? Nothing?" He's got a look of shock on his face. "Really?" he repeats.

"Really. And why is that so hard to believe?"

"Well, with the hair, and your ex—"

"How do you know my ex?"

"From orientation last year."

Gosh, that was right after Stan first left me. It was one of the few times he'd come around, to go to the parent orientation. After, he took Fleur out for ice cream while I sat on the couch and cried, both for my baby going to kindergarten and for the life I'd lost.

"How do you remember that?" All I remember is the tears. And the feeling that I'd never, ever be ready for her to go off to school. Yet here we are, and I'm surviving. Sort of.

"You stand out, you know. You're certainly not like the other moms."

"Because I'm so witty with my dry sense of humor?"

Ross gives me a blank look.

Okay.

"No, the hair. It makes you stand out."

"I'd like to think it makes me memorable."

"That too. I certainly remembered you."

I can't help but feel flattered.

Ross continues. "Yeah, everyone was talking about that TV show, and then how you were getting divorced."

Awesome. The fluttery, flattery feeling is starting to dissipate. This "play date" is not off to any better a start than my horrible date with Ted. What the heck? "Well, you seem to know about me. What's your story? You know, with you and Zoe's mom."

"You know the story. Woman says she's on the pill; she's not really. Nine months later ... surprise!"

"Oh, wow that sucks." It's hard for me to believe that someone would actually do that, but I guess I don't really know people anymore.

"Yeah. I wasn't really planning on the whole kid thing."

"With her or ever?"

"Ever."

I'm waiting for him to say something about how now he wouldn't change anything, or how Zoe is the best thing that's ever happened to him, but Ross simply continues ranting about Zoe's mom. Gosh, I hope I never sound like that when I'm talking about Stan, no matter how much he deserves it.

"So, really, are you going to tell me about your tattoos or what? Why are you playing coy?"

Dude, why is he so fixated on this? I don't have tattoos, and there's a very good—and personal—reason. I made a pact with my brother that since he couldn't get one, I would never either. Now I know Jimmy probably wouldn't have held me to it all this time, but a promise is a promise. Ross doesn't deserve to know that about me. And he won't stop about the dang tattoos. Since he can be blunt, so can I, and say as much to him.

He scooches his chair a little closer to mine. I wish we weren't sitting at the island. "I dunno. I guess I sort of have a thing for bad girls."

"What makes you think I'm a bad girl?"

Ross pulls back and looks me up and down. I'm wearing a turtleneck, but in this moment, I sort of wish I had a lead suit on. "You know, the hair. The eyebrow piercing. I know you've got to have some hot ink under that nun's outfit."

Suddenly, there's a crash, followed by a cacophony of screaming from Fleur's room. I'm off my stool and down the hall before I know it.

"Mommy! She ruined it." The tears are already starting to stream down Fleur's cheeks. And then I see it. Her overturned doll house. "She broke my house! Daddy's house!" And then Fleur dissolves into full-on hysterics.

"It was an accident," Zoe offers with a shrug.

I push by her to take Fleur into my arms. She's inconsolable. "Daddy made that for me, and it's all I have from him."

I glance down at the overturned house. The porch railing is crushed on one side, and the chimney's fallen off.

"How did this happen?"

Zoe casually strolls over to Ross. Again with the shrug. "We were playing tornado. It's what happens when there's a disaster."

"Zoe, there's a difference between pretend playing and destroying someone else's stuff," I say.

"Oh don't worry about it, Zoe. No need to get upset. These things happen," are Ross' words of fatherly wisdom.

Still holding a sobbing Fleur, I rise to a stand. "You know, Ross, I think it'd be best if you and Zoe go."

Ross looks at me. "Really? Why? Kids play. Things get broken. No big deal."

Is he kidding me? His kid comes in and goes all Godzilla on my child's most prized possession, and he thinks it's no big deal?

"I think it's best. It's going to take a while for Fleur to calm down."

"I guess. Maybe we can do this again some other time."

Over my dead body.

"Yeah, sure. Maybe."

I don't even show Ross and Zoe out. My mom's house isn't that big. I'm just thankful Mom wasn't here to see this. I can picture her going psycho on Zoe. Frankly, it takes everything I have not to open up a can of you-know-what myself.

Trying to suck air in as she cries, Fleur says, "It's ruined, and it'll never be good again."

There's quite a bit of broken wood. I remember how many nights Stan spent locked in the basement, assembling the Victorian miniature house. We should have known when it came in a flat box that it would be labor intensive. Night after night, Stan would go downstairs, only to come up a few hours later rubbing his eyes and muttering, "Some assembly required." I didn't understand at first, until I went down and saw the bazillions of little pieces, all needing to be glued together. Each shingle on the roof was separate. And for Stan, with his baseball-mitt-sized hands, working with those tiny parts was painstaking.

And now, it's in pieces.

I want to cry too.

"Don't worry, honey. I'll fix it. I'll make it better."

"How?"

"I'll get the glue gun and put it back together. Like Humpty Dumpty."

"But all the king's horses and all the king's men couldn't put him back together again."

She's too smart for her own good.

"Okay, not like Humpty Dumpty."

After a while, Fleur finally calms down, the occasional sniffle escaping. I look at all the parts and wonder how long this is going to take. Good thing I get an employee discount at House of Crafts. I'm going to need a lot of glue sticks.

My first instinct is to call Stan for help. Obviously, since he built it, he knows how things go together. But then I remember that I don't have that option any more.

I wonder if he'd come if there was really a crisis. I don't even know where he's living right now. With being on the road so much, it would be easy for him to set up shop practically anywhere on his route. Would he do this for his daughter?

Since I don't know the answer, I decide not to ask the question.

Before I even know what I'm doing, my fingers are pulling up my contacts.

"Tony? It's me."

Chapter 20

The fact that Tony didn't answer doesn't stop me from leaving another long, rambling message. What am I doing?

This is what's been running through my head since Saturday night. Maybe the business of the week will distract me from what a moron I am.

I'm volunteering in Fleur's class today. Probably a good thing, since she's been so clingy all weekend. She seems almost disproportionately upset about the house, especially since I've started reconstruction. It's going to take a while. I think I may hate that Zoe girl. We are so not doing another play date.

Before that night, I'd had a sliver of a hope there might be something there. Until he started talking of course. It's not enough that he's cute and gets the single parent thing. It doesn't counteract the weird vibe he gave me from insisting I have tattoos. Seriously, what was up with that? It was so bizarre. Being a dad isn't enough to make up for his personality. Just because he's a single parent doesn't mean he gets how I want to parent. I can't think simply because someone pays me any iota of attention that they have potential. Nope, no potential there, just a wasted night, expensive chicken nuggets, and a broken dollhouse. Oh well, it goes with my resolve that I don't need to be dating. Tony, then Ted, now Ross. Maybe it's not them. Maybe it's me.

That's it. I'm defective. My husband didn't think I was wife material, and I'm obviously not dating material. At least I'm mom material. That's where I'll focus my energy.

The classroom activity involves making handprints. Seriously, who thinks it's a good idea to paint the hands of twenty five-year-olds? I'm guessing that's why the teacher lined up two volunteers. I can't help but think the other mom, Colleen, is giving me the stink eye when she thinks I'm not looking. Little does she know I'm always looking.

Maybe I'm simply being oversensitive. My ego's taken quite the hit lately, so it's not that far-fetched I might imagine people are gossiping about me. Plus, Ross pretty much said so. One positive memory I have of my dad is him saying the best defense is a good offense. Time to go on the offensive.

"This project is so cute, but I don't think I'd be brave enough to try it."

Colleen looks at me, a bit startled I'm speaking to her. "Oh, I know. Should we place bets on who spills the paint first?"

I'm not quite sure who Colleen's kid is, so I certainly don't want to pick the wrong kid. "I'm guessing it will be me. I can make quite a mess when I'm in the creative zone."

Colleen laughs. "Oh, me too. I'm the worst with flour. It's why I don't like to bake. The recipe might call for only a spoonful of flour, and somehow it looks like a snowstorm hit the kitchen."

"Oh, my gosh, me too! I call flour my arch-nemesis!"

Colleen gives me a smile as Mrs. Hammond begins giving step-by-step instructions. It seems complicated to me, with the kids moving from table to table. I'm at the painting station. Colleen is on hand-cleaning detail.

"Better you than me. I'd be afraid I'd miss a spot, and someone would put a handprint somewhere."

"Mrs. Hammond knows I'm a freak about things like this."

"As long as it's not flour!"

The first gaggle of kids comes up, and I have to focus on painting hands orange and red for fall leaves. The project is actually super cute, and I'm thinking about framing Fleur's. I pretty much think everything she brings home is frame-worthy. The pile of papers I've amassed from the first few weeks of kindergarten is staggering. Multiply that by twelve more years of school, and I'll be living like a hoarder.

My hour of volunteer time is up before I know it. The kids are ushered off to gym, and Colleen and I are kindly but distinctly asked to leave. I get it. It's Mrs. Hammond's lunch, and she doesn't want to get sucked into endless conversations about how great our kids are. At least, that's what Colleen tells me as we're signing out. It makes me feel a little better, because I had been hoping to check in on how Fleur's doing. There's been so much transition this year that I'm afraid it will manifest itself somehow.

"Do you have plans right now? Would you like to go for a cup of coffee?" Colleen's invite takes me by surprise.

"Um, I was going to do something totally exciting like hit the market, but I can probably make that sacrifice."

We head over to the Starbucks and order our drinks. Once at the table, Colleen starts. "So, how are things going for your daughter? Is she your first?"

"Um, yeah. Well, only. I never planned on her being an only, but I'm guessing that's how it's going to be."

With a raised brow, Colleen says, "Oh?"

"Yeah. My husband, well, I guess he's now my ex-husband ..."

"Say no more. I'm sorry. Is this recent?"

"Yeah. Well, a few months now." I try to think back. It's the first week in October. He left at the end of April. Wow, I've survived five months without him. "Over five months. He's moved on. Frankly, he'd already moved on before he left. That was a technicality."

"How about you? Have you been able to move on yet?"

I think about my dating disasters. "I'm trying. It hasn't gone so well. But honestly, I don't think it's because of Stan. He's been so terrible that even if he came crawling back, I wouldn't want him. I just suck at dating, I think."

"It's been so long since I've been on a date that I don't think I'd even know how to do it anymore." There's a wistfulness to Colleen's voice.

"That's where I'm at too. Stan and I had been together for fifteen years. I never thought I'd be out here again."

"Fifteen years? That's how long Kent and I have been together."

"So, yeah, it can happen. I hope it doesn't, because it sucks royally."

"It does. But you've already tried dating? That's good that you're back out there though."

"Yes and no. There's this one guy, but he's way too young for me, plus he lives in New York. No way in heck I'm doing the long distance thing. Then I had a disastrous date with some guy I met at a bar. Do you know what 'Netflix and chill' means?"

Colleen takes a sip of her latte and shakes her head, so I fill her in. "And then, Ross, Zoe's dad, sort of indicated that maybe he was interested, but the play date went south quickly."

"Oh, Ross. Stay away from that one."

"Really? He seemed friendly at first, although I'm not sure about Zoe. I guess I did get a bit of an odd vibe from him." I obviously have no intention of dating him, but I want to know the dirt.

"Yeah, I'm telling you, stay away. He's a serial dater. He prays upon the single moms, and some of the not-single ones too."

"Yuck."

"Yeah. He's a creeper."

"You know what was weird? He kept asking me about my tattoos. He was super-fixated on them. Like he kept asking to see them. It was a huge turnoff."

"Why?"

"Um, because I don't have any. I don't know why he thought I did, but he was pretty insistent."

"That is weird. But I would have thought you had some ink, to be perfectly honest."

"Why?"

Colleen stalls by taking another sip of her drink. Her eyes dart around the cafe for a moment. "Oh, you know, the hair."

Reflexively, my hand combs through my hair, pushing it back off my face. "Because it's colored?"

A flush rises up on her cheeks as she nods. "Yeah, it's pretty punk for the suburbs. There was talk about tattoos and piercings. Most of the moms who have ink keep it conservative. Every so often, someone dares to show their ankle tat. We're pretty boring here."

It makes me immensely uncomfortable to know people are talking about me. I want to run and hide and never show my face at school again. My face must betray my feelings as Colleen quickly continues. "It's no big deal. We're a pretty boring lot. Your hair is so cool that it spurred lots of talk. I think most of the moms were wishing they were cool enough to do it. And we were wondering what else you were cool enough to do."

Now it's my turn to stall by drinking the last bit of my coffee. "I've been doing the hair for years now. Probably before it was trendy. I just like color."

"Yeah, but you pull it off so well. I'd look like a moron. You look hip."

Her words do little to reassure me. All I can think is that the other mothers are talking about me. What else are they saying? The thought that they're speculating about my body is too much for me. Let's face it, I like the fact that people look at my hair and not my body. It's sort of the opposite of camouflage.

But now, after talking with Colleen, the last thing I want to do is stand out. For the first time in my life, I'm starting to think that maybe making a statement isn't a good idea.

Whether I wanted it or not, I have a new life. Maybe brightly colored hair doesn't fit into that anymore.

Chapter 21

"Are you sure?"

"Yes, Emay. I'm sure. A cut and color."

Through her thick black frames, Emay glares at me. "But why? And why now?"

"It's time for a change."

"I don't know that I can do this."

"If you don't, I'm going to Quick Clips."

Emay clutches her black tunic and stumbles back. "Don't say those words in here."

"I'm sure they'd be happy to take my money and do what I ask."

"Fine. I'll do it. Let me go and mix up the color."

Though I thought I was sure about what I'm doing, I still can't watch while Emay applies the dye to my hair. Nor when she takes the scissors and starts cutting away. But I can't ignore the tears forming in Emay's eyes.

"Is it that bad?"

"No, of course not, because nothing I do is bad. It's ... it's just ..."

"What?" I'm impatient waiting for her response. Her stammering is getting on my nerves. I'm not normally like this, but I'm so apprehensive that I can't handle Emay's emotions too.

"I loved doing your hair. It's one of the few times I could be truly creative."

"Hell's bells Emay, I'm just going back to brown. It's not like I'm shaving my head."

"Hell's bells? That sounds like something my grandmother would say."

"As long as you don't give me her hair, I'll be okay."

Two hours later, I'm all set. I have to say, Emay is truly an artist. If I ever had to put on a runway show of my designs, or do a photoshoot, I would want her. She's a genius.

And I now have a mom-bob.

It's not really a mom-bob. It's still an inch or two below my shoulders, falling in soft waves. The color is a rich chestnut that matches the brandy coloring of my eyes. I look so ... normal.

Which is what I want. I've wanted to go shorter for a while. This is a good move. A positive thing. A new hair for a new me. For my new life. A life where I focus on being the best mom I can be. I should probably figure out the job thing too, because I don't know that I can work at House of Crafts for the next thirty years, but a career change seems too daunting right now.

One step at a time.

And see? No mention of men in there, which is a good thing. I don't need that hassle right now.

"I actually sort of love it. I didn't think I would, but I do."

"That's because you're sort of a genius. I was just thinking that if I ever got my design business up and going, I'd have you do all my styling for the models."

"Are you going to do anything with that?"

I shrug. "Dunno. Too much to handle at this point. And as much as I like designing, I'm still burnt out from the show. It really sucked out my creative energy."

"Not to mention after the show." Emay takes off the cape as I shake my newly shortened locks. It feels so odd to have the ends of my hair just grazing my shoulders.

"Oh yeah, Stan definitely helped with sucking out my creativity. I can't believe how light my hair feels."

"The brown covered up the color nicely. If the light catches it the right way, you may still get a hint of the blue. The purple doesn't last nearly as long. This will give your hair a chance to grow back in without stripping it for a while."

"It looks so, so ..."

"Normal?"

"Yeah." I can't keep the resignation out of my voice. I've no creativity left, and that even shows in my hair.

"Kira—it looks great. And you'll rock this just as much as you rocked all the colors."

I wish I had her confidence. I knew there was a chance that losing on *Made for Me* might knock me down a few notches, but it's been everything else in the past few months that's really put me down for the count. I need to start pulling myself up again. But how?

Turns out that somewhere in the cosmos, some being must hear my pleas of desperation. Before I'm even back home, Michele begins blowing up my phone.

I don't answer the first call, because I'm driving. Then the text message alerts start coming. On her second call, there's a cop sitting behind me at the stoplight, so I can't answer it. More text notifications. By the third call, I'm pulling into my mom's driveway, so I can answer it.

"Are you on fire? If so, you should probably call 9-1-1. Otherwise I can't think of what is so important that you have to call me a billion times in ten seconds." Perhaps I've been listening to the arguing-style of a five-year-old for too long, since that sentence is totally impossible.

"I am practically on fire. Oh, Kira, you need to help me! Please say you will. I don't know what I'm going to do if you can't help me!" Michele's practically in hysterics. I've seen her reach the hysterical phase. It's not pretty. I've got to talk her down NOW.

"Whatever it is, we'll handle it. What did Christine say?" I know that as frantic as Michele is, she's most likely already run this by her BFF Christine.

"She told me to call you. I am so screwed."

If Christine's pointed Michele in my direction, it's gotta be sewing related. Christine is super-organized, which Michele needs since she's the poster child for ADHD. "What's going on?"

"Well, I have to go back to Montabago. There's a thing that Maryn needs a dress for. So, I've been working on some sketches and stuff, and I sort of forgot about my Etsy, and when I checked today, I've got a bazillion orders."

"I thought you were shutting it down?"

"I meant to, but I forgot."

"So, cancel the orders. Problem solved." My stomach twists a bit. I'd like to think it's because I'm hungry and not because I'm filled with jealousy that so many people want her stuff.

"I was going to do that, but what does it say about me? It says I'm unreliable, and people don't want to do business with unreliable people. It will be bad for my brand. People are willing to wait for custom-made clothes, but this is getting ridiculous.

"True. I'm guessing that's Lincoln's input." I try not to remember that Lincoln and Tony are roommates. Or at least they were until Michele moved down to New York. Frankly, I'm not sure what the living arrangements are at this time. I hope they didn't kick Tony out. That would be wrong. Geez, my attention is no better than Michele's.

"Well, yeah. He's part of my team and all. And that's where I need you."

"Huh?" Sometimes it's hard to follow Michele's train of thought. Especially since I'm now sorting through the mail and see a large manila envelope from the county clerk that can only contain one thing—my final divorce papers.

"I want you to join the team. To officially be a part of New Michele Designs."

"What am I supposed to do for you? You're in New York. I'm here in Columbus. It's too much of a commute."

"Shipping is shipping. You can ship from anywhere."

"Shipping?" I really am not following. Dang, I'm officially divorced. I've been saying it for a while and have considered it to be so, but seeing it in black and white from the Franklin County Clerk is so ... final.

"Yes, shipping."

"Michele, I'm not following you. What am I shipping?"

"I thought that was implied. I want you to help me make the clothes. To fill these last orders. All billion of them. I don't trust many people with my designs, but I know you would make them like I make them. I trust you to keep with my aesthetic."

Okay, she's got my attention. "Seriously, how close to a billion are we talking?" I've seen some of her pieces on Etsy. Skirts and dresses mostly. They're not super complex, but are custom made for the specific measurements of each customer, which might take a little more time per garment.

"I don't even know. I stopped looking at five hundred. I've started making them, but I have to go soon, and there's no way I can even make a dent."

"Five hundred? Holy crow. Even if you did two a day, that's still over eight months."

"I know. I don't know what to do. If I did two a day, and you did two a day, and we could find a few other people, then it could be manageable, right?"

"Okay, well, I'm guessing Asher and Lexington are out, but what about Weyler? She might help."

"I can call her and see. So you'll do it? I'll pay you."

"Of course you're going to pay me. I work, so if I'm doing this, I can't do both."

"Even before this came up, I was going to see if you wanted to come work for me anyway. Would you be the lead at New Michele? I know you don't live here, but I can come out to you, or you can come here every so often. I didn't want to ask this way, but it seems the universe had other plans. It seems to have other plans for me a lot. Like with Lincoln and—"

"Michele, you're rambling. Write up a proposal, and I'll let you know about this being a permanent thing. In the meantime, send me the fabrics and patterns, and I'll start filling the orders."

And just like that. New hair; new job. Funny how that works.

Chapter 22

"May I help you?"

"Mrs. Hammond, it's me. Kira Noles. Fleur's mom. I'm scheduled to be the mystery reader today."

I've been trying to do something with Fleur's class as much as they'll let us into the classroom. I'm scheduled for a field trip next week too. Right now, time is at a premium. I decided not to totally quit House of Crafts and instead reduced my hours by half. And I sew. Early in the morning. Late into the evening. Mom's in on it by helping package up and ship out the garments once done.

"Oh, yes of course. I ... I didn't recognize you."

"I've been getting that a lot lately."

She looks me up and down. Not in a bad way, more pensive than anything else. "Why?"

"I would think because all people ever noticed was my hair. Now that it blends in, they have no idea who I am."

She smiles, her face showing a well-worn pattern that tells me she uses this expression a lot. It's a good sign for a kindergarten teacher. "No, I meant why did you stop coloring your hair?"

I wish I had some snappy answer, but the truth will have to do. "Some of the other moms—and dads—were talking about me, and I'm not sure I want the attention for that reason."

"Yeah, the gossip mill can be brutal."

"I've had a rough enough year. I don't need to go looking for more trouble."

"Well, for what it's worth, your hair now looks nice, but I liked it the other way too. It had pizzazz."

"I thought so too but well, you know."

"This looks very becoming on you as well. Own it."

Funny, I thought a kindergarten teacher would only be able to relate to five-year-olds. Maybe Robert Fulghum was right in saying that everything you need to know you do learn in kindergarten.

I'm getting used to the shorter length of my hair now. I can't wrap it up like I used to in a top knot on my head, but I can, at least, pull it back into a ponytail when I'm working.

"Well, in any case, I'm glad you're here. The children will be delighted, Fleur especially. Did you have a book in mind to read?"

I show her my well-worn copy of *Ferdinand*, which promptly brings a smile to her face.

"One of my favorites."

"Mine too. My mom's, actually."

"That's perfect."

My time in kindergarten goes much too quickly, and before I know it, I'm heading back home to sew. Michele's put a freeze on the Etsy site, so at least no new orders will be coming in. I'm able to make three pieces on a work day and about five on a day off. It's easy being this productive when there's no thinking involved. I follow the pattern and adjust for the measurements. Once you've made one red pencil skirt, it's easy to put on the repeat button. I don't want to admit it, but I like all the sewing. On the other hand, I'm exhausted.

It's good though. Because it keeps me at home. I don't have time to date or to think about dating or to wonder if I should be dating.

Except, on those rare nights when I don't pass out from exhaustion, I'm lonely. Sure, Stan was gone a few nights a week on the road, but I was used to having someone here at least some of the time. That's all I want. Someone to snuggle with, to share my stories with, to laugh with.

Oh crap, I want to date again.

Except I really don't. I don't want to meet people and be all awkward and stuff. I want the comfortable fit I had with Stan. Yes, I know things are all exciting at the beginning, but I know what comes next is even better. That's what I want. But now, I have neither the time nor the energy to put into this endeavor. And since Tony won't even return my calls or texts, that ship has sailed. I'd be starting at square one, and I don't have the energy for that right now. Oh sure, I know that Michele's project won't last forever, no matter how much it may seem that way.

Let's face it, in the past three weeks, I've made about ninety skirts. At this rate, I'll finish with the skirts in about three months. I hope by that time, she's caught up on the other orders. For a website with only four designs, I can't believe how popular it's become.

Obviously, it's because she won *Made for Me*. It's what we all hoped for by going on the show; that a win would parlay itself into a better career. I'd hoped for a production offer by a major label for some of my designs. I mean, how cool would it be to see your name on clothes in Macy's or even Kohl's? I know a lot of designers would pooh-pooh that, because it's too commercial, but commercial is where it's at. I'm not a fancy person. I'm okay having my name in a chain store. I would prefer it, actually.

But now it's a moot point, because no one's going to offer me squat. I'm a well-rounded loser.

At least I'm consistent.

No time for wallowing. I log onto the computer to check the order status. Christine put together a spreadsheet on google that we can all access. It's color coded, and even though I would never come up with something like that, it makes me happy. It's so pretty. Christine definitely has her stuff together. All this, and she's in the middle of planning her wedding. Michele is so lucky to have her. She'd never make it otherwise.

Slowly but surely, we're making progress. Weyler is working on it too. She's doing the jumpsuits. They take a bit more work, so she's not able to fill orders as quickly. There aren't as many of those, so it's a good balance. She's in New York too, so she uses Michele's studio space for her work. Christine's in Upstate New York, and Michele's back and forth to Europe. New Michele Designs is a global operation at this point.

I'm happy to be a part of it.

My messages ping, and I see that it's Michele. She normally texts, so this should be interesting. I hope it's not one of those things that you're supposed to forward to nine people within thirty seconds or the sky will fall. I hate those.

It's a meeting notice. In New York. She can't be serious. I mean, I could try to Skype in. Maybe that's what she wants.

I respond as such.

Nope, she wants me in New York. She's got new things to run by me, and she thinks it needs to be done in person. I don't know how I'm going to make that happen. I have responsibilities here. I have House of Crafts. I have volunteering at Fleur's school, not to mention her dance lessons. She wants to start ice skating this winter too. I can't just take off on a whim and jet to the city.

It's a make-it-work moment.

For once, I wish my life wasn't full of make-it-work moments and that things would fall into place nicely. That doesn't seem to be in the cards for me, at least not now.

The first thing I need to do is see if I can get the time off work. Management has been generally good with me because they're using my presence in the store and my ties to *Made for Me* for promotional purposes. They're planning a big campaign for Christmas, including me doing some classes. The extra financial stipend is certainly incentive, and the more I do, the more I make. In theory, with enough of these events, I wouldn't have to have actual hours at the store.

I don't want to wait until tomorrow to talk to Marty the Manager (that's how Jani and Morris refer to him), so I head to the store before it's time to pick Fleur up at school.

"What's up? You're not quitting are you? You can't quit. We just made the posters." Marty the Manager picks up a large piece of cardboard from behind his ever-cluttered desk. They'd taken my picture before I re-colored (un-colored?) my hair. I think the design looks a little cheesy, but it certainly is eye-catching. Loud colors splash the advertisement, promising a Q&A and sewing lesson with me.

"No, I'm not quitting, but I might need some time off from my regular hours. I promise it won't affect the events."

He sinks back in his chair, perspiration evident. "Sure, whatever you need. The first two events are sold out already."

This makes my stomach flip a bit. People want to come and see me. To listen to me. To learn from me. That's pretty cool. "I'm committed to them. I have to go to New York for some meetings with Michele."

"*The Michele?*"

As a sewing addict, Marty the Manager goes totally gaga at the mere mention of Michele's name. When he found out I was sewing for her business, I thought I would have to break out the smelling salts.

"Yes. It's part of the big order I'm working on. I don't know why, but she needs me there in person."

"Whatever she—I mean you—need. Do you think—"

"I'll ask."

"How do you know what I'm going to say?"

Because he's fangirling—fanboying—so hard right now that it's not even funny. "I'll ask Michele if she wants to do an appearance here. She hasn't really done anything like that. I'm not sure if there are contractual restrictions with the show or not, but I'll check it out."

"OMG, that would be ..."

"Marty, you're not a sixteen-year-old girl. You can't say OMG."

"Maybe I'm a sixteen-year-old girl at heart. You can't deny me my true self."

I flash him the 'whatever' sign and turn to leave.

"Oh, Kira? One more thing."

"What now Marty?" He'd better not ask me for signed underwear or anything. Michele and I are close, but not *that* close.

"You are going to dye your hair back for the events, right?"

Chapter 23

"But you CAN'T go!" Fleur is wailing again. Like throwing her body on the ground, literally kicking and screaming. She hasn't had a tantrum like this in years. She's always been so easy going. Even her twos weren't terrible.

"Fleur, I have to go. It's business. It will only be a few days. Three at the most."

That doesn't help. I didn't realize it was possible for her to scream any louder, but oh yes, she can. Her face is bright red and turning perhaps a bit purplish. It's a distinct possibility that she may pass out soon. I can't let that happen.

"Fleur, sssshh. It's okay, baby." I scoop her writhing, twisting mass into my arms. In order to avoid being kicked, I put her in what basically amounts to a wrestling hold, restraining every part I can. She's getting long and lanky, and this isn't as easy as it used to be. Her wails have dissolved into indistinct sobs and sniffles. I have no doubt my shirt will be covered in tears and snot by the time this is all done. Funny, at one point in my life, that would have bothered me, but the only thing that bothers me now is the obvious state of upset my daughter is in.

Murmuring into her hair, I continue to rock Fleur and assure her that she's going to be fine.

Through gasps for breath, Fleur manages to get out, "But ... Mommy ... you can't ... leave me ... too."

My mom enters the room, and we lock eyes at this statement. My heart, so tenuously held together, has just shattered into a million pieces. Of course I can't leave her. I can't let her feel, even for one moment, that I might be gone for good. I don't know how long it will take me to rebuild that feeling of security in my daughter, but if I have to spend the rest of my life doing it, then I will.

I could kill Stan for this.

"It's okay, baby. I won't go. I'll call Michele right now and tell her I can't come to New York."

My mom lifts the now-calm Fleur out of my arms so I can manage that piece of business. I don't know how this will impact my role at New Michele Designs. I guess I'm basically a dressmaker at this point, so I'm sure they can find someone to replace me.

And again, a massive feeling of resentment washes over me. Stan's the one who did this by leaving and doing it the way he did. Now that I might actually have an opportunity and am doing something fulfilling, I have to give it up. Don't get me wrong, I will make any sacrifice I need to for my daughter, but this is all because Stan is a selfish jerk.

"Hey Michele, it's Kira. Um, I've got an issue with the meeting next week, and I don't think it's going to happen. Call me back when you get a chance."

I don't know where Michele is at this point, so I'm not sure when I can expect to hear back from her. I feel bad letting her down, but there's really no other choice. From a purely selfish point of view, I was looking forward to going back to New York for a few days. I love that city and was hoping to draw upon some of its creative energy.

Within about five minutes, my phone starts ringing. "Kira, this is a disaster! You can't not come! You have to be here!" Michele's voice is about three octaves above glass shattering, causing me to hold the phone away from my ear.

"Michele, I'm so sorry. I can't."

"Why? Why can't you come? What's more important than this?"

Her comment immediately makes me bristle, but I have to remember that Michele doesn't have kids, so she doesn't know.

"Fleur. She totally freaked out when I told her I had to go away."

"Why? You were away before, and she was fine."

"Yeah, but that was before Stan left. I think she's afraid that I'll go away and never come back too. I mean, she's only seen him three times since he left. I don't anticipate it getting any better. I think she's thinking that if he can leave, then so can I."

"Oh, poor baby. That's so sad."

Tears threaten. I've vowed to shed no more tears over Stan, but this is really about my daughter. "I know. I have no choice. I understand if it means I can't work for you anymore. You have a business to run."

"What? What are you talking about? I wouldn't not work with you because you're a mom. That's

161

insane. In fact, if I knew Fleur was having such a difficult time, and you left her anyway, I'd be super pissed at you."

"So, can I Skype in then?"

"Yeah, no. That still won't work. I'll have to see what I can figure out. This is going to be problematic."

"I thought you said it was okay?"

"Well, yeah, it's what you have to do, but it ruins everything on my end. Let me see what I can figure out. I'll be in touch."

Fleur's reaction, followed by the phone call with Michele, does nothing to make me feel better. It's not fair that I don't get my life. It's not fair that my daughter is so insecure. She's probably going to have issues. I know I did after my dad left. As I entered my twenties, it became my choice to cut off any relationship with him, not that he bothered that much. I was older, but it was still hard to realize the problem was with him and not with me. I have to keep telling myself that about Stan too. It's him, not me.

It's hard not to feel that it's me.

Mom's finally got Fleur settled down. She's in her room, drawing. She's an incredibly artistic child and will choose a creative outlet over TV any day. Lately, it's been imaginative play with her newly repaired dollhouse—the family had survived a tornado. I know that might change as she gets older, but I hope it doesn't. She fills my heart with joy, watching her create. After I tuck her in and retreat to my own room, I try to hold onto that. It's a tiny glimmer, a small light in the darkness that fills my chest.

If I just knew why Stan cheated on me, why I wasn't enough, then maybe I could work on improving that part of myself. How was I so lacking? How did I not know that I was letting him down so much?

If I were speaking to Stan, which I have no desire to do, I would ask him. I know I'll need to put all my anger aside and communicate civilly with him for Fleur's sake, but he's pulled such a disappearing act lately that I haven't had to test that particular skill. I certainly can't imagine a point where we'll be having any kind of heart-to-heart about the downfall of our marriage. So maybe I don't know what was wrong with me, but I know without a shadow of a doubt that there is nothing wrong with our little girl. For him to walk away as he has, to replace a wife and child with that— I shouldn't use that sort of language—only tells me one thing.

There's nothing wrong with me. There's nothing wrong with Fleur. The problem is with Stan. The realization hits me like a ton of bricks and brings on a flood of tears. For once, they're happy tears instead of sad ones. Well, there are a few sad ones mixed in, because I loved Stan. I truly did. The past few months have certainly cured me of that. I could never love a person who treated me the way Stan did. But it doesn't make me feel any better. I miss having someone to love. I miss being loved.

And Tony pops into my head.

Dang.

I glance over at the clock. It's after one a.m.

Whether I want to admit it or not, one of the reasons I was looking forward to New York was the chance I might see Tony again. I haven't really heard from him—other than a few vague texts—since that kiss in front of Stan. My constant analysis of the situation tells me Tony was upset at my behavior because maybe he had some interest in me. Which means I probably hurt him and blew any chance I may have had.

I was sort of hoping I'd have a chance to mend that fence. The realization that I won't get to see Tony brings on another round of tears. My pillowcase is soaked. I should get up and find a new one. Instead, I roll over to the other side of the bed. If I have to sleep alone, I can at least take advantage of the extra space.

The morning brings a new day but not necessarily an improved frame of mind. How many things can I be expected to give up while Stan has sacrificed nothing?

Mom, who's a professional at reading my mood, places a cup of coffee in front of me and starts rubbing my back. She's done the same for as long as I can remember, and I find myself doing the same thing to Fleur.

"You know what sucks, Mom? I don't have a choice anymore. I have to do what's best for Fleur, even if it's at the expense of my own needs."

As soon as the words are out of my mouth, I want to suck them back in. Mom was in the exact same situation twenty years ago. "Oh, Mom, I'm so sorry. I know you did the same thing for me. I'm sorry you had to."

"I am too, but I'm more sorry that you're in the same situation. It's taken me a long time to forgive your father. Sometimes, I still don't think I have."

"I don't think I can say that I *forgive* Stan, but I also realize it's his loss, not mine. He's the one missing out."

"It took me a very long time to get to that point. You're in much better shape than I was."

"Is that why you never really dated after Dad?"

She shrugs and turns away. She's not usually one to avoid, so I know I've hit a nerve. "Probably, now that you mention it. I was too afraid to get back on the horse."

For some reason, that brings all sorts of wrong images to mind, so I try to stay serious as I push visions of my mother and a cowboy out of my head.

"I think it's why I was trying to help you out with that Tony-fellow. I'm just so happy you put yourself out there again."

"A fat lot of good it did me. And you know, that's part of why not going to New York has me bummed out. I was maybe hoping to see Tony again. But I can't leave Fleur, so it's not even an option."

Mom turns around with a wicked grin on her face. I don't trust that look. It usually means she's up to no good.

"What?"

"I've got a plan."

Uh oh. Mom's up to no good. I'd better watch out.

Chapter 24

"In theory, it's great. In reality, no."

"When did you get to be such a negative Nellie?" Mom's smug smile is fading in light of my rejection.

"When my whole life went to crap. I have to start being a realist. And, unfortunately, my reality is not super positive right now."

"Maybe if you were putting a more positive vibe out into the universe, it would come back to you."

"Are you going all hippy Karma on me? I don't think I can handle that right now."

"No, I'm asking you to be positive and think about it before just saying no."

"It won't work."

"Why not? If you can't leave Fleur, then bring her with you. Problem solved."

"I can't. I'm not going to sightsee. I'm going to work. And I don't even know what the work is. It could be long hours, late nights. What is Fleur supposed to do all that time?"

Mom's silent for a minute. I'm done with my coffee and just staring at the empty mug. She's still flitting around, tidying up things that don't need to be cleaned. Finally, I hear her still. "Well, I could come too. That way Fleur and I can do things when you're busy."

In a perfect world, it makes perfect sense.

We all know my life is anything but perfect.

"Like I said, it sounds great, but it won't work."

"Why not?"

I'm not sure how she doesn't automatically get the logistics. Or, more accurately, the financials. "There's no way I can afford it. Michele would pay for my flight out there, and I'm sure I would crash with her. But if all three of us go, that's two more flights, plus hotels, cabs, meals, and entertainment. I don't have that kind of money to spare right now, not heading into the holidays."

"I'm sure I could—"

"No, Mom, I'm not letting you spend your money on this. You've worked your butt off my whole life, and now you're letting us live here, and you won't even accept help with the utilities or rent or anything."

"You buy most of the food."

"We eat most of the food. It's like, literally, the very least I can do."

"Kira, don't be so hard on yourself. You've done a great job getting on your feet, and I'm sure you will continue to do well. Yes, this would set it back a little, but isn't it worth it?"

I run through the pros and cons in my head. "I wish I could say for certain that it is. But I don't know, because I don't even know what Michele has planned. It could be world-changing, or it could be something minute. With Michele, you never know."

Mom nods. She's met Michele. She's wonderful and creative and energetic, but organized she is not.

"Maybe you can call her and get some more information so you'll know if this is worth it."

I stand up, clearing the last of my place. "I would, Mom, but I don't think she would understand why I need to know. I think she gets why I can't leave Fleur, but I don't know that she would understand the money part." Michele, by her own admission, is neither savvy nor responsible with money. She had to give up her apartment and sell most of her things to pay off some debt before going on *Made for Me*. She can relate to family responsibility, but I don't know about the fiscal part. "It was a good idea, but I don't see it working."

Gloom colors my mood for the rest of the day. I wish I could justify spending that sort of money. I even look up flights. On one week's notice, the best I can do is over five hundred dollars for each flight. That's a thousand dollars just to get Mom and Fleur out there. Nope, can't do it.

I turn off the computer and sit staring at the blank screen. My phone pings, indicating yet another text from Michele. I text her back that I'd been looking into bringing Fleur and my mom but can't afford it. Wow, this sucks. I know Michele won't judge me, but I feel ashamed nonetheless.

She doesn't respond, probably distracted by something in her glamorous life. About thirty minutes later, my phone finally dings. An email. Wasn't expecting that.

And what I really wasn't expecting was a flight itinerary. Or I should say, itineraries. One for me, one for Fleur, one for my mom.

I hit the call button with record speed. "Michele! You can't do this!"

"It's already done, and they're non-refundable, so now you can't say no."

"I can't let you do that."

The other end of the phone is silent. I have to look to make sure I didn't drop the call. Finally, she says, "Too late. It's a done deal. So now the only thing is to think about what fun things you're going to do while you're here."

"I thought I'd be working? Aren't I pretty much an indentured servant at this point?"

"Since you all are coming, we thought it would be best if you came for a full week so you can get some sightseeing in. Fleur's never been here, right? There's so much to show her. We're going to have a blast!"

Michele's enthusiasm is contagious. Before I know it, I'm booting my computer back up and googling family-friendly things to do in New York City. "Michele, I can't thank you enough!"

"You say that now, but this is a work trip too. Don't forget that!"

"I won't. I just wish you'd tell me what it's about though. I could mentally plan a little better if I knew."

"Plans, schmans."

It figures Michele would say that.

"I thought you had a team of experts making sure you have plans and structure for everything now. Isn't that what Lincoln and Christine and Lynn do for you?"

"Yes, they're keeping me on the straight and narrow."

"Will they all be there?"

"No. Lynn's about to burst, she's so pregnant. I didn't think it was possible for someone to get that huge, but my sister's done it. I think eating a loaf of bread and a container of hummus every day in the first trimester didn't help."

"Yikes. No, that's not a good idea."

"Yeah, she wised up and tapered on the weight gain, but now the baby is huge and she has nowhere to put it."

"Right, because she's tiny. When's she due again?"

"In two weeks. The week of Thanksgiving."

"So you're hoping to get all this business done before the baby's born?"

"That's my hope so I can head home and see the new peanut as soon as he or she arrives."

"I still can't believe they didn't find out the gender. I wanted to know as soon as I found out I was pregnant with Fleur."

"Yeah, it's a thing in our family. No one finds out. It's like a superstition or something. And you can't buy anything for the baby before it arrives either. That's an Italian thing."

"Remind me never to marry an Italian. I'd never be able to do that."

"Awww, I can't do that. It would automatically take Tony out of the running. He's like, pure-bred Italian."

"He's also a kid and lives six hundred miles away from me. I don't think he was ever in the running."

Not to mention that I act like a freak of nature whenever he's around and have done everything humanly possible to drive him away.

"I don't think any of that matters to Tony. In fact, I'd say that I know it doesn't."

"What's that supposed to mean? Were you talking about me? Did he say something? What did he say? Oh God, I don't want to know."

"He—"

"No, I don't want to know. I mean, I totally do, but I can't want to know. It's not a feasible thing, so I can't hear about it."

"Does that mean you want it to be a thing? Are you interested in him?"

Gosh, she's blunt.

"Michele, he's twenty-five. I'm thirty-five, almost thirty-six. I have a daughter. I'm at a different place in my life right now."

"Yeah, yeah, yeah, all that. But are you interested in him?"

"He's hot, he's funny, he's smart, and the most delectable kisser. Of course I'm interested in him."

"Good." And with that Michele disconnects without saying another word.

Oh no, what did I just get myself into?

Chapter 25

"Mommy, are we there yet?"

I thought kids only did this on car rides. The plane's barely hit altitude, and Fleur's already about to bust out of her skin. I kind of feel the same way, but for many different reasons. At first, she was happy to get out of school for a few days. I value education, but traveling can provide as much education as a week of kindergarten, right?

My dealings with Michele have been strictly business since that one phone call, but I can't stop thinking about it. Tony must have been talking to Michele about me, right? She didn't sound negative. She seemed encouraging, not discouraging, so the things he was saying had to be positive. Either that or I'm the world's biggest fool.

I'm guessing the latter.

In spite of this, I can barely contain my excitement. It's pitiful, actually, since I have no inkling when I might even get a chance to see Tony. And, even if I do, I've got my mom and daughter in tow. If that's not a huge reality check, I don't know what is.

I'm sure it'll be enough to drive him off.

My trepidation fades as soon as the plane lands. Fleur's excitement is contagious. Even my mom has a huge grin on her face. I made sure to hide her smiley-face pants before we left, so they don't make an appearance on this trip. The Big Apple isn't ready for them.

We're waiting for our baggage while I fiddle with my phone, trying to get an Über, when I hear a familiar squeal.

"KIRA!!!!!!!!"

I look up to see Michele barreling toward me. "Oh my God, what did you do to your hair? I barely even recognized you!"

My hand flies reflexively to my head. I'd forgotten that it was no longer a vibrant color, just a sensible brown. "Oh yeah, I probably should have warned you."

"Why?"

"Well, so you'd know what to expect."

She gives me a playful push. "No, why did you stop coloring it? Why brown?"

One of our bags approaches us on the conveyor, so I take the opportunity to lean away from Michele to grab it. I know she doesn't mean to be insensitive. She's always saying whatever pops into her head. It still burns a bit though. And just as I'd gotten used to my new hair.

Since Michele is now distracted again, I take the opportunity to introduce her to my mom and Fleur as we wait for the remaining bags. They don't take long, and Michele leads us out to where she has a car waiting for us.

"You hired a car?"

"Well, for something as special as this, yes. I've actually become good friends with the guy who owns the service. His husband works with Lincoln, so we've been using them a lot. Sometimes it works better than a cab, especially coming from LaGuardia."

"You're really moving up in the world."

"I'm trying to be responsible with the money. Lincoln helps me with that." In addition to her booming business, there was also a sizeable cash prize from winning the show. It pops in my head again that if I'd won, I bet Stan would have tried to get half of it. Thank goodness I didn't have to deal with that. Plus, if I'd won, I don't know how I'd manage all the travel with Fleur. Maybe the universe knew what it was doing when I didn't win. And, let's face it, Michele deserved it. Her ideas are fantastic. I absolutely support the judges' decision. I'm also in full support of Michele getting help with her finances. Getting together with Lincoln is one of the smartest things she's done.

"He's good for you." I place Fleur's booster seat in the car and slide in next to it. I get her buckled in as Mom and Michele take their places.

Michele turns herself around from the front seat. "The right man can do wonders, if you know what I mean."

Even if I didn't know what she means, the heavy waggling of her eyebrows tells me. "If only it were that easy, Michele."

"You're telling me? Do you know what a colossal mistake I almost made with you know who?" Her voice drops to a loud whisper, like she's trying to be discreet.

"Michele, my mom watched the show. She saw the footage. She knows who. And yes, it would have been a colossal mistake."

"So, we don't want you to make the same type of mistake, if you know what I mean."

"Yes, Michele, we all know what you mean."

"Oh, that. My aunt Maria says that all the time. You know, Tony's mom."

I've suddenly got a very bad feeling about this whole trip. "Michele, I'm going to say this once, and once only. I'm here because of the business. I hope to God that there's actually business, and that this isn't some sort of elaborate set up to try and get Tony and me together. My life has been torn apart this past year. I truly can't handle anything else."

She looks stunned. I've never been short with her before, but I don't think she'd have picked up on any subtleties at this point. Abruptly, she turns around, returning to facing forward. I look at my mom who gives me a frown. Fleur's oblivious, thankfully, as she's mesmerized with the buildings and the people outside the car.

"Mommy, look at that! And that! Did you see that?" Her five-year-old wonderment makes me happy for a minute, letting me temporarily forget the trepidation that had been overwhelming me just moments before.

I need to stay in the moment and focus on her. She's what's important. This is her first time in New York. I was in high school before I came here. My friends and I drove practically all night to arrive in the city in the early morning hours. I was with two friends, but we only had two tickets to go see David Letterman.

I ended up drawing the short straw. I walked around while they were at the show and got harassed by some homeless lady looking for money, claiming she could get me a fake ID.

I'm hoping Fleur has a better time than that.

At least I hope she's not yet considering a fake ID. Kids grow up a lot faster these days.

There's a lot of stop-and-go traffic as we approach Midtown. It makes me want to throw up a little. I glance over at my mom, and the greenish pallor on her face makes me think she's feeling the same way.

"Um, how much longer until we get to your … where are we going?"

"We're heading to the hotel to drop you off first. I figured you'd want to get settled. Then, I'll be back to pick you up, and we'll be heading to the studio."

"Is that far from the hotel?"

"No, they're both in the East Village."

"And where do you live in relation to that?" Mom chimes in.

"I'm pretty much in Alphabet City."

"Oh, right," Mom murmurs. She has no idea about the layout of the city. For all intents and purposes, Michele could have told my mom she lived on the moon.

"Alphabet City?" Fleur pipes up. "Is that where Sesame Street is?"

God, I love that kid.

"It's hard to find, but I think Sesame Street is in Queens." This is from the driver. I didn't even know he was listening.

"Well, that's dumb. Cinderella should live in Queens. Sesame Street should be in Alphabet City. Are the buildings shaped like letters at least?"

"No, sweetie. I hate to disappoint you, but the buildings are shaped like buildings. The streets are letter names. Avenue A. Avenue B. Like that." Michele has turned around again to address Fleur.

"I feel robbed." Fleur crosses her arms and goes back to looking out the window. It's hard not to laugh at her. I wonder for the millionth time how Stan could be so stupid to walk away from her. We haven't seen him since that debacle with Bambi and Tony. I'm sort of okay with it.

The car finally stops at a large glass building rising from the concrete. It's got a bit of an asymmetrical shape with an additional structure about a third the size morphing out of it. I think it's part of the same complex, but in New York City, you never can tell. "Where are we?"

"This is where you're staying. The Standard. It's super cool. You'll love it."

Michele is right, and I'm afraid to know what this room is costing her per night. She shouldn't be doing this. She's going to blow through all her money before the year's out. I tell her as much as we're staring out the eighteenth-floor window overlooking Manhattan.

"Don't worry about me. I'm good. This is the very least I could do for you. I wouldn't have won if you hadn't helped me. Heck, I'm not sure if I would have made it through the show if you hadn't been behind the scenes giving me words of advice, even though we were competing."

Thinking back on the romance-related advice that I gave to Michele, it makes me chuckle. "If that's not irony, I don't know what is, me giving you advice on romance."

"I actually think your advice was to not get romantically involved."

"And see, I was right. Asher was not the right guy for you."

"Could you tell that?" She's speaking in a hushed tone so my mom and Fleur can't overhear. Of course, at the moment, Fleur's flopping around in the bathtub, making plans for a massive bubble bath.

"Yeah. Obviously."

Her face falls. "I can't believe I was so dumb."

"You weren't dumb. He's handsome and charming. I'm not sure I'd be impervious to his charms if he'd focused them on me. But he's slippery."

"Slippery?"

"Yeah, slick. He's a player."

"I can't believe I almost picked him instead of Lincoln."

"He would have screwed you over so bad. I'm glad you came to your senses and made the right decision."

Michele pulls me into a tight hug. I think she might be crying. Oh, brother. "And that's all I want for you. I want you to come to your senses and make the right decision."

I pull back. I'm not a hugger. "But you see, no matter how much you may want it, I don't know that Tony's the right person for me. Even having a fling with him was too complicated; we can't even seem to do that right."

"You're going to see him while you're here, right?"

I turn my gaze back to the stunning view. I don't know how to answer this. I don't want to encourage Michele. I'm afraid she'd take any response in the affirmative direction and run with it. She doesn't understand what's at stake and why I can't just jump into something with someone simply because I find him attractive. Not to mention that we haven't spoken in over a month.

"Mommy, Grammy says she's going to use all the bubbles and there won't be any for me!"

"Mom, stop teasing her. It's not nice." I stoop down and pick her up. "Grammy's trying to be funny. There are plenty of bubbles to go around. Michele and I are going to go to work for a while, and you and Grammy are going to explore."

She buries her head in my shoulder and tightens her grip. "Please don't go!"

"I'm going to work for a while. We're going to meet up for dinner." I look at my watch. "It's in three hours. You can make it three hours without me, right?"

"Not a minute more." She takes a stern tone with me that is well beyond her years.

I grab my bag and coat, and Michele and I head for the elevator. I hope she doesn't bring up Tony again. Even if I wanted to be with him, I don't think I could deal with her reaction to us being together.

"What's the plan for the rest of the day?"

"We're heading over to the studio."

"Is this when I finally get to find out the big news that I absolutely had to come to New York to hear?"

She looks at her feet. "Um, that'll be tomorrow, I think."

"Do I need to know anything about it ahead of time?"

"You should look nice and do your hair. I still can't believe you colored your hair."

"Um, Michele, I've been coloring my hair. It wasn't purple and green naturally."

"You know what I mean." We walk through the lobby and back out to the waiting car. It doesn't take long before the car stops again. This time, we're heading into some super-sketchy-looking building that could either house hip, high-end lofts or drug dealers. Maybe both. Either way, I sort of want to break out into the soundtrack from *Rent*. I don't think Michele would appreciate my rendition of "La Vie Boehme," even though I know I kill it in the shower.

Her studio space is the former with windows that span floor to ceiling, letting the natural light pour in. The sun splashes on bolts of colorful fabric standing up against a table. The only time I've seen this much fabric in one place is when it's for sale. By the wall opposite the windows are boards and boards of drawings. Pinned up, overlapping, some flapping. They're stunning, and once again, I'm taken aback by Michele's talent. It's blossomed and grown exponentially since the contest.

"This is incredible. I could … it's just … wow."

"I know, right?"

Chapter 26

I could spend hours—days—in a space like this. No wonder her creativity is exploding. Maybe something like this is what I need to get back into the groove of designing and creating.

"Gosh, I can practically feel the creative energy in the air. All I want to do is design."

"I was hoping this space would help with that. I also had to make it a distraction-free zone when I'm working. No electronics, no talking. You know me. It takes everything I have to stay focused."

"Yeah, but once you get working, you get into a zone. Like you're super focused and the world doesn't exist."

"That's been a problem too, since I tend to lose track of time when I'm working. And since I turn my phone off, Lincoln can't get a hold of me. It drives him insane."

"Yeah, but he loves you anyway. It's not like he didn't know this about you."

She gets a dreamy look on her face, thinking about Lincoln. I glance away, lest feelings of envy consume me. "Okay, so what are we doing? Do we have a project to start or what?"

"Oh, I forgot, I've got a meeting. It won't take long. Why don't you hang out here? If you get bored—but I don't think that will be an issue—you can work on orders. There's a list over on that board, and all the stuff is here."

With that, she breezes out the door. I don't like her tone, and have a sinking feeling in my gut. She's set me up.

My suspicions are confirmed when I hear the old freight elevator come back up to the floor. I don't need to turn around to know it's not Michele coming back up because she forgot something. I should have known this whole thing was a set up. Why can't she leave well enough alone? I'm quite capable of making a mess of my own life.

"Don't be mad."

I still won't turn around. I'm trying to breathe and count to ten and not totally lose it.

"Please." His voice is so soft and pleading that immediately my resolve melts, and I turn to face him. His boyish good looks stun me again. I try to focus on the boyish aspect, but I can't. Every fiber in my body wants to run to him.

"Is there even a reason that Michele really needs me here?"

"Yeah, there's a legit thing coming."

I cross my arms, trying to hold myself back. "Do you know what it is?"

Tony doesn't answer. His head is cocked, and he's staring at me. Not me, my hair.

"What?" I'm holding onto the last bit of defiance I have. If he makes any negative comment about my hair, I'm so out of here. I'll grab Fleur and my mom, and we'll drive back to Columbus if we have to.

"I didn't think you could get any more beautiful."

Well, dammit. Heart meet floor.

Before I can stop myself—heck, why would I want to *stop* myself—I run across the studio to Tony's waiting arms. It's not our first kiss, but it feels like it is. The world begins to melt away, and the feelings of doubt and uncertainty fly out the window. I could get lost in this man for a very long time.

He pulls away slightly. Good God, why is he stopping?

"There's no one watching, right?"

"Um, I don't think so. We're the only ones here."

"So you're not doing this to hurt someone else."

"No, but if you don't start kissing me again, I may hurt you."

"Just checking."

And his lips are back on mine, where they should be. Why have I been fighting this? It feels so right. He feels so right. I'd forgotten how firm his back is. I pull him tighter, my breasts pressing into his chest. This action causes him to take notice of them, and he begins trailing his kisses down my neck and into my ample cleavage.

The girls—not to mention my whole body—have felt neglected over this past year and are enjoying the attention. *I'm* enjoying the attention. From the feel of it, so is he. I close my eyes, letting the feeling of the moment take me away. There's a couch over by the far wall, and I start slowly moving toward it, hoping I don't trip over anything and maim Tony and me in the process. He glances up. "Do you want me to stop?"

"Good God no. I'm trying to get over to that couch." I nod, indicating to the inviting piece of furniture on the far wall.

He grabs my hand and practically runs for the sofa, pulling me down on top of him as soon as he sits on it. Next thing I know, my shirt is off, and he's attending to the girls again. I'm fumbling, trying to get him undressed without making him stop. It's not working so well.

Tony's sexy mouth works back up to my own, and I can resume unbuttoning his shirt. Even though he's obviously in good shape and I'm not, for once, I don't feel self-conscious shedding my clothes in front of him. Maybe it's because I'm not wearing Spanx. In fact, by some stroke of luck (or the subconscious thinking that I wanted and expected this to happen), I'm actually wearing a pretty decent set of matching charcoal-gray bra and panties. At my size, sometimes pickings are slim, so this is one of the nicer things I have.

Shirts off, hands and bodies tangled together, I'm feeling pretty dang good about life. He grabs my hands, and for some reason, the feeling of his hands on mine seem to short circuit my brain. I cannot think of anything but having this man. Right here. Right now. I lose all sense of judgment. All I can think about is having him. Now.

Tony pulls back for a minute, and I'm terrified he's going to stop. Instead he whispers, "I know I've waited this long for you, but I'm not sure I can wait one more minute."

Before I know it, his hands are ripping off my bra. Then it's time for the skinny jeans, which seem sexy until you're trying to peel them off without falling over. Tony starts fumbling a bit. I put my hand on his to stop him.

"Don't worry, I've got this." With one swift movement, I've taken care of the pants issue and can now focus on him.

"Okay, but we've got to make this quick. I don't know when someone might walk in."

"Tony, it's been months and months. It's gonna be quick."

You know, quick doesn't mean bad. I'd forgotten how good a quickie could be.

Then he says, "I can't believe that just happened."

FOR THE LOVE OF GOD, I'M GOING TO KILL HIM. Why does he keep doing this to me?

"No. Wait, why?" Thoughts flood my head. Just when I was feeling super sexy and confident too. I bet he was totally turned off by my fat rolls. Crap.

"I can't believe that happened." Not like I needed him to repeat it.

Yup, he's totally disgusted by me. I will not cry. I will not cry. I will not ... damn.

"Oh my God, Kira, don't cry. Please, honey." With the most gentle touch, he wipes away the tear that is spilling down my cheek.

I try to cover myself up so he can't see the grotesqueness anymore. I'm trying to get off his lap, but his one hand is still around my waist, pulling me into him. I must look like a beached whale flopping about on the sand. I need to get my clothes and now.

"Kira, I only meant I can't believe we did that here. It's my cousin's office. It's kind of gross."

Disclaimer: I may or may not be in a rational state of mind at the moment.

"Did you just call me gross?" Because, of course, that's all I hear. I finally tear myself off his lap and find my shirt. How did it get halfway across the studio? I cannot believe this is happening. Again. Why did I expect something different this time around? And why the heck are skinny jeans so much harder to get back on than off? I'm hopping up and down, trying to wedge myself back into them. Not a pretty sight.

And how could I have pegged Tony so wrong? Why would he and Michele go to all this trouble if he didn't really want to be with me? Did he lose some sort of bet? My mind is instantly transported back to all those 80s movie clichés, and I just know I'm one of them.

"Kira stop. Now." His voice is full of authority, and despite my cray-cray behavior, I find myself obeying him. And maybe a little turned on.

"What?"

"I said that having sex in my cousin's workspace is gross. At least, I know I'd be grossed out if she and Lincoln did it in my office. Mostly because I don't have an office; I have a cubicle, and I know my perverted coworkers would be watching. But still, I don't want her nekkid body in my workspace, so we should keep this quiet."

Oh.

He probably thinks I'm crazy. I did lose my mind for a minute there. "Oh. And I probably just blew it by going all psycho for a minute. Any chance you can develop temporary amnesia?"

"You keep talking sexy like that, and I'd be willing to forget it."

"Huh?" I'm so smooth.

"All that talk about blowing things." He moves closer and winks.

"It's not like it's really an office. We didn't do it on her desk or anything. I bet she never even uses this couch." I can't believe that happened. Never have I ever been so rash. Good Lord, what did I do?

"Okay, so it's probably not as bad as it seems. Still, I want the next time to be a little more private."

He wants there to be a next time? Maybe he's not totally disgusted by me. He leans in and kisses me again. I still don't have my pants all the way on. If he keeps kissing me like that, we're not going to get to anywhere private. Once fully dressed, I pull out my phone.

"Is this really the time to be calling someone?"

"Not calling, texting." Luckily, Mom responds quickly, confirming that she and Fleur are uptown by Central Park and won't be back this way until dinner. "My hotel room is available until about dinner time. My mother and daughter won't be back before then. I want to do that again."

He looks down at my feet. I've finished lacing up my fashionable hiking boots that in no way could ever handle hiking up a mountain. "Oh thank God."

I look down, trying to figure out what reason he has to be grateful about my feet. "Thank God what?"

"Your shoes. I'm guessing you can walk pretty fast in those. I was afraid you'd be wearing silly girl shoes, and it would take us forever to get to your hotel."

I can't help but smile. I don't get how, with only a few words, he can make my insides go all mushy. Probably because I don't want to wait one more minute for him either. "Nope, I can walk. And walk fast."

And walk fast we do. Actually, if it weren't for the fact that I don't really know where I'm going, I think I would have beaten Tony back to The Standard. The elevator ride up to the eighteenth floor is slightly uncomfortable. There's part of me that wants to go all *Fifty Shades* and start at it hot and heavy. But then there's the realist that knows this is a public space and, given our track record, something would go drastically wrong. I manage to control and contain my passion until we get back to the room.

Once the door is opened (and locked and dead bolted—not taking any chances here), I can no longer contain myself. And neither can Tony. And, for once— well, twice—we finally manage to take our time and get it right.

Chapter 27

"Mommy, Mommy, you should have seen it. There were big huge rocks. As big as buildings. And I climbed all the way up to the top!"

"That's great, baby. I bet you're tired after all that walking." Fleur climbs up and sits on my lap. She's paid little attention to Tony in the ten minutes since they've been back. I'm not sure if it's good or bad.

"No, I'm not tired."

"That's too bad. I am."

"Well, why are you so tired? You didn't go anywhere. You're still in the hotel room."

I give Tony a sideways glance, and it takes every ounce of strength I have left—which is not much—to resist laughing. I don't want my mom to know either. I mean, it's okay that she knows Tony and I are, well, whatever we are. But I don't need to go announcing the post-coital bliss I'm currently feeling.

"I think it's time for us to go now. Michele and Lincoln are meeting us there." We're all heading to some pizza place in Little Italy. Tony insists that Mom, Fleur, and I need to go there to experience real New

York pizza. This afternoon, as we lay entwined in bed, he told me about all the places I need to see here. For a moment, I wished I could pick up everything and move to the city to be with him. I know it's not a real possibility, so I try to stay in the moment and not think about anything but how amazing he makes me feel.

Fleur poops out before the pizza arrives. She's nestled into my side, and eventually her head ends up in my lap. Tony looks at me and then pulls his phone out. My phone quickly buzzes, and I try to read it as discreetly as possible. Basically, he's said he wishes he could be in Fleur's position. I hope the dark atmosphere of the restaurant conceals my blush.

I choose the mature way to handle the situation, so I ignore him. "So, what are the plans for tomorrow?"

Mouth full of piping-hot pizza, Michele exhales a few times, trying to avoid burning the roof of her mouth. "I do this every time," she mumbles with a full mouth. "It's too good to wait for it to cool down."

I carefully slice off a small piece with my knife and pick it up with my fork. I gently blow on it a few times and then pop it in my mouth.

"What the heck are you doing?" Tony's mouth is agape.

"Um, eating?"

"What are you eating?"

I really don't see why this is a big mystery. "Um, pizza. Just like everyone else."

He clutches his chest and collapses backward against the booth. His head is down, and for a split second, I'm worried that he is choking or something.

Lincoln pipes up from across the table. "You just committed the number one cardinal sin in Tony's book. Well, besides rooting for the Red Sox."

What could I have done so wrong? "If eating is a cardinal sin, he'd better rethink this. I mean, one look at my butt should have told him that I like to eat."

Still slumped, Tony mumbles, "It's not *that* you eat, it's *how* you eat. Pizza. With a fork. I can't even."

I look at Michele and roll my eyes, thinking it's funny that he's adopted her frequently used phrase. Personally it drives me bonkers when she uses it. Especially when she "literally can't even."

"What can't you even?" I look down at the next bite of pizza on my fork. "What? This? It's hot. This cools it down more quickly so I can eat it faster."

"You cannot eat pizza with a fork!" He's upright now, and his eyes are wild.

"Wanna make a bet? Watch me!" And I pop that perfectly cooled piece of pizza in my mouth. "See? Perfect temperature. No burn on the roof of my mouth. No need for the reverse blow." I nod at Michele when I say that, as she's doing it again. "Just cut it up. It's better this way."

Tony reaches over and takes my face in his hands. He pulls me toward him, well as close as he can without disturbing the sleeping five-year-old pinning me down. "Kira, I think you're very special. I think what we have is very special. But I'm telling you, for the love of God, if you eat pizza with a fork, it's a deal breaker."

I can't do anything but look into his eyes, and I'm almost positive he's dead serious. While I don't like to wait to eat my food, if this means that much to him, then I guess it's a sacrifice I can make. "Okay." I try to nod but his grip won't let me.

"Promise?"

Holy cow, he is totally serious. "I promise."

He leans in, kissing me slow and sweet. It's almost easy to forget that I'm at a table with a bunch of other people, including my mom. Until Michele starts clapping. "Awwww, I'm so happy for you guys. You finally got together and figured it all out!"

When she says that, it triggers an alarm bell in my head, because even though we have gotten together so to speak, we haven't truly figured anything out. He's still too young. I still have a daughter. And we still live six hundred miles apart. Tony must see the panic flashing through my eyes. He leans in even closer and whispers, "Don't panic. We'll figure it all out."

I nod and he lets me go. "Okay." I hope he doesn't notice how unsure my voice sounds.

"Are you really okay?" Dang, he did notice.

"Yes, I am. But I need one thing."

"What?" He's nervous, I can tell. I don't want to get into it here.

"How am I supposed to eat my pizza when it's too hot if I can't use my fork?"

He puts his arm around me. "Stick with me. I'll show you what you need to know."

"Awwww. Okay, enough of the lovey-dovey stuff. Now it's time to get to work." Michele's attempting to command attention. She's not successful, as the conversations are continuing. I should try to pay attention to her, but I only want to look at Tony.

Mom's talking to Weyler, and Lincoln is typing furiously on his phone.

Tony's ... Tony's looking at Fleur, still snuggled in my lap. He's got a slight smile on his face, giving him a dreamy look. It's usually the look I see women get when they hold a baby. Oh no, this cannot be happening. I am in no way, shape or form mentally prepared for this. I don't know why I thought I could do this.

Dating isn't about me anymore. It's about Fleur too. I have to think very carefully about what this might do to her. She's already sort of messed up because of Stan. I cannot let guys traipse in and out of my life. That would totally give her the wrong message. I should be more like my mom, who showed me the important thing was not to have a man but to be an independent woman.

Gosh, I never really thought about it until now. That's totally what she taught me. What am I doing here then, making out with this guy I barely know in front of friends and family? Not to mention what happened earlier!

My first instinct is to slam my head down on the table, but there's not an inch of spare space. So I do the next best thing: I try not to hyperventilate. I press my eyes together and focus on breathing in for four and out for eight. I open my eyes and see Mom looking at me, concern evident on her face.

I hope no one notices that I'm quiet for the rest of the meal. Suddenly, I'm as tired as my daughter and wish I could put my head down and sleep. And when I wake up, not have to face the train wreck I'm making out of my life.

The meal ends without event, and I finally have to move Sleeping Beauty. As I struggle to do so, Tony picks her up and settles her head down on his shoulder. Fleur snuggles right in, and her eyes stop fluttering, returning to their peaceful state of rest. I think my ovaries may have exploded a little.

Mom, being Mom, announces almost too loudly that she's going to go for a walk before returning to the hotel. I believe she really wants to—she's always been active—but I know she wants to give me time with Tony. I don't know whether to love her or hate her for it. I don't want to get into it tonight. It's been such a great day, and if all I have is this day, I want the memory of the whole day to be wonderful.

And, if I can get out of my own head, it is wonderful. Tony's funny and sweet and sexy. Except for when he freaked out about the pizza with a fork thing—and of course the whole Spanx incident—I can't find a flaw. Walking home, Tony's carrying Fleur as if he does this every day—what more could a girl ask for?

So why, then, am I so convinced that this will never work out?

Chapter 28

"What happened?" Mom calls from the bathroom.

"With what?" Her question is out of the blue, and I have no idea to what she is referring.

"With Tony."

Oh, please. I do not want to have this conversation with her. I mean, we're open, but there have to be some boundaries. In some ways, I'm relieved that she never dated after Dad left, because I'm sure she would have shared—and overshared—details that I have no desire to know. "Um, what do you mean?" Playing dumb is always a good strategy.

"At dinner. You two were all smushy face, and then you freaked out."

The mere mention of it is enough to send me back into hyperventilation. "What do you mean? I'm not freaking out. I mean, I wasn't freaking out. Why would I freak out? There's nothing to freak out about. Everything's fine."

"Obviously not." She walks out of the bathroom, ready for the day. She's got on sensible mom jeans and white sneakers and a striped sweater. Sigh. I'm not sure where I got my fashion sense from, but I'm almost sure it wasn't her. "Stop judging my outfit. It's practical for walking. And you're totally freaking out. Still. Why?"

I sit down on the bed. Fleur's entranced by SpongeBob. I hate this show with a passion. "Because Tony."

She sits down on the foot of her bed. "Well, duh. Of course because of him. But what happened? Something must have."

I take a deep breath before starting. "The way he was looking at ..." I nod my head toward Fleur, not wanting to tip her off that we're talking about her. "He had that little goofy smile that baby-crazed women get when they hold a baby."

"Do you think he's interested in you to get to her? Like in a pedophile way?"

"Oh good God, no! In fact, that's never even crossed my mind. No, family's really important to Tony. You know he's Michele's cousin. They're all very close."

"Then why would it freak you out? I'd see that as a plus."

"Because what if he really likes her ..." I nod again, "... and she really likes him, but then it doesn't work out between us? I'm messing her up. I don't want to see her on *Intervention* or *Hoarders* because I totally ruined her life."

"Don't you think you're being a bit dramatic? When did you get to be this pessimistic? I mean, it's not like you were ever bubbling over with positivity, but you're starting to be depressing. At least when you're with Tony, you're not such a Debbie Downer."

"Gee, thanks, Mom. Your support is overwhelming." I stand up and huff off to the bathroom to finish getting ready. I start brushing my much shorter, much more mainstream hair. My hair sucks. I hate brown. Stupid parents at school making me feel badly about myself.

"See? I can see your scowl from here."

"My hair sucks."

"No, it doesn't. It's very becoming on you."

"I look boring."

"You look like me." She's joined me in the bathroom and is standing behind me. It's true, I do look a lot like her, just as Fleur looks like me. "Are you calling me boring?"

"Oh no, how could you be boring wearing jeans with a smiley face patch on the butt? That's not boring."

"Don't hate on my happy pants. I know you hid them, by the way. They make me happy. I wear things that I feel comfortable in and make me happy. I don't care what others think of me. All that's important is how I feel about myself. You should remember that."

I put the brush down on the counter. "What if I don't feel good about myself?"

"Then you need to figure out what does make you feel good and do that."

Mom lets me finish getting ready. Michele told me to look "fashion forward" today, but I'm not feeling it. I've got on my favorite black leather pants with a black godet top, a cropped denim jacket, and slouchy suede black ankle boots. I add a large flat silver necklace and earrings. It looks so dark. I wish I had something for a pop of color. I used to rely on my hair to add that color. Without it, my wardrobe seems dark and dull. I've got to start working on that.

I give Fleur a tight hug and say goodbye to Mom. They're doing more exploring today, including lunch at the Russian Tea Room. It sounds like fun. Tomorrow, I'm surprising Fleur with a visit to the American Girl store. It should keep her well occupied for the trip home the following morning. I can't wait to see her face when we get there. I figure if I had to take her out of school and totally mess with her routine for a few days, there should be a fun reward.

The walk back to Michele's studio doesn't take me long on this brisk November morning. Thinking about her space, I can't help but remember what transpired there with Tony, and then what happened after as well. I don't know that much about him, but I do know we have chemistry. Unbelievable chemistry. I lose control of my senses, both the good and the bad ones, when I'm with him. Like there's some magnetism pulling me toward him. I had an inkling of that eons ago with Stan, but it was never this strong. And that scares the living bejeezus out of me.

As soon as I arrive at Michele's studio, I know I'm in for a big surprise. The studio is crawling with people and cameras. I recognize some of the crew from *Made for Me*. Oh no, what is Michele up to now? To quote Han Solo, I've got a bad feeling about this.

"Kira! You're here! Oh my God, I'm so excited! I can't even!"

"Michele, what can't you even? What's going on? What is everyone doing here?"

Even Callie Smalls, the host from *Made for Me,* is slinking about, moving as only a super tall, super thin, supermodel does.

"This is why you had to come! They're doing a follow-up and are helping with my new announcement."

"I still don't understand what it has to do with me though."

Michele knots her hands together and lets out an evil little laugh. "All in good time, my pretty."

"Yeah, you don't do a good Wicked Witch imitation. You're more like Glenda."

"Whatever. You'll find out soon enough. Oh, this is so exciting!" And she skips—yes, literally skips—away.

I make small talk with some of the crew. A few of them don't recognize me until I start talking. Apparently they remember my dry voice more than my face. I never realized how much people looked at my hair without looking at me. I always thought my hair made me memorable. In fact, in some ways, it made me more forgettable. Interesting.

The action is starting, and we're getting wired for sound. I haven't missed this at all. I didn't enjoy being on the show. It was quite stressful, and I'm not that competitive. Obviously. Plus, other than Michele, I didn't socialize much. I didn't care for many of the other contestants, and I assume the feeling was mutual. Weyler's all right. She didn't bother me at dinner last night, and we've been in occasional contact since we're both working on Michele's massive Etsy order.

Callie Smalls I could do without. She is not warm and friendly. I mean, I'm not necessarily either, but she's downright frigid. Maybe it's because she's too thin. Maybe she's perpetually hungry. I know how grumpy I get when my belly's empty. I never once saw her at the craft services table, even when our days on set were long. Lucky for me, she doesn't want to make small talk. Or any talk for that matter. I wonder why she took this job in the first place, since she doesn't seem to enjoy it.

Finally, the lights are where the lights should be, and the sound is working the way it should be working. Weyler and I are positioned at one of the work tables, while Michele is at another table, perpendicular to us. Or us to her. However you look at it, when they shoot Michele, we're in the background. I lean toward Weyler. "What are we supposed to be doing? Sitting here? Are we supposed to look busy? Otherwise, I think we look stupid."

"I don't know, but I feel like we should be pretending to sew or something. We do look stupid just sitting here."

I'm trying to talk without my mouth moving. "Do you know what this is about?"

"No clue. You?"

I shake my head. "Do you think it's about the order? Why is the crew here? Are we here to make her look good for the 'Where Are They Now?' episode?" But that doesn't make sense. If she had needed me to make her look good, she would have said so. It wouldn't have been such a hush-hush thing.

"You think?" Weyler can raise her eyebrows freakishly high.

"No, I don't, but I don't know what else it can be."

We get a look from one of the sound guys. Apparently we're making too much noise. Okey-dokey.

Callie saunters in front of the camera and begins her spiel. "Welcome to this very special follow-up episode of *Made for Me*. Today we're catching up with the winner, Michele Nowakowski, at her fantastic design studio in New York City. Let's see what she's been up to since the show wrapped."

Callie turns to Michele, who's never been great in front of the camera. This could be disastrous for her. "I, um, well, you see, I did the wedding stuff and then, well, I, um kind of forgot to close my Etsy shop—but it's closed now, so please don't try to order. I mean, thank you for all your orders, and I'm sorry if you want to order, but my next thing should help out with that."

It's like watching a train wreck. Michele is incredibly smart about sewing and designing. But she can come off as a bit ditzy. That's mostly because she's got a pretty substantial case of ADHD. I wonder why she's not medicated. At least for something like this. I hope the editing team can do something with what she just said so she doesn't end up looking like a flake. That couldn't be good for business.

Callie tries to catch that train barreling down the tracks. "And I understand that you have an announcement you'd like to make?"

"Oh, yes. I'm so excited. As you can see—" I see Michele point to us. I can tell how hard she's trying to rein herself in and possibly even imitate Callie Smalls a bit. "I've brought in Kira Noles and Weyler Axelrod.

You see, what happened, as I already mentioned, is that I forgot to take my Etsy store down, and I got absolutely flooded with orders. Too many for me to possibly do myself. So, I hired Kira and Weyler to help, and the girls and I have been powering through the orders. That's part of the reason they're here."

I shift on my stool. I want her to get to the point. When Michele's nervous, she has a tendency to forget what she's already said and start repeating herself. She's doing that now.

"Anyway, selling New Michele Designs through Etsy doesn't work, because there's too much demand for the supply. So, drum roll please ..." Michele looks expectantly at Callie, who simply looks annoyed. "Um, okay, my big news is that I've partnered with Cleo's Department Store to create my own line of women's clothes. It will include standard, as well as a petite and women's line." A huge smile spreads across her face.

I want to cry, but the cameras are still rolling. I'm happy for my friend. Well, I will be once I've drowned my sorrows in a large vat of ice cream and beer—separately, not together. That would be gross. Not only did she win the show, but now she's literally living my dream. I close my eyes and take a deep breath and pray that the camera doesn't pan to me. I can't look at her. I can't even look at Weyler, whose body goes rigid next to mine. Why on earth would Michele bring us here for this? She doesn't have a mean bone in her body. And we've been helping her out. Why would she do this to us?

Callie jumps in. "That's wonderful news, Michele. Can you tell us a little about what we'll be seeing in Cleo's and when?"

"Things are happening so fast, you know? Plus, I'm still under contract for Mar—I mean Princess Maryn—through the spring, so I think the earliest possible that my collection will be available will be late fall or winter. As you know, my signature is relevant retro. But I know that look doesn't appeal to everyone. So, I've decided to bring on two other designers to balance out the collection. Kira will be handling our modern edge collection, and Weyler will be in charge of our working women collection."

And now the camera does pan to us, just in time to catch Weyler's mouth fall open, and me fall off my stool.

Chapter 29

"Kira, how do you feel about Michele's announcement that you'll be a co-designer for her fall collection at Cleo's Department Store?"

Even an hour later, the shock still hasn't worn off. "You could have knocked me over with a feather."

"Oh, is that what happened?" The producer tries not to laugh. "Tries" being the operative word.

"For all intents and purposes, yes. I had no idea why Michele wanted me here. She went through a lot of trouble to get me out here. It was all a big surprise."

"I'll say. At least we have you in more for this portion of filming."

Yeah, they've got me on the couch where Tony and I hooked up yesterday. Gosh, was that just yesterday? I feel like I've lived five weeks since then. So many ups and downs and ups. My adrenaline has spiked again. I'm all jittery and can barely sit still. I can't wait to tell Tony. This is possibly the biggest thing that's ever happened to me. Mmmm, Tony. Gosh, that was so hot. I wish we could do it again right now, minus the cameras of course. Oh crap, I'm pulling a Michele. I need to focus.

"I'm sorry, what was that you said?"

The producer looks annoyed. "I said, what we really want to know is, what happened to your hair? Did you lose a bet or something?"

I'm taken aback by his tone. "What do you mean?" No way I'm letting him off the hook on this one.

"Why did you color it?"

"Well, Chris, I've been coloring it for years. This is simply a different color than the one you last saw me with."

"The brightly colored hair was your signature look. It's what made you edgy and modern. I mean, your collection is called Modern Edge by New Michele Designs. How are you going to be able to follow through on that?"

I tilt my head, and I'm almost certain my face has contorted to give him the stink eye. "Well, Chris, I'm not Samson. My strength is not in my hair. I still have talent."

"But why would you want to get rid of the very thing you're known for? Aren't you afraid no one will know who you are now?"

He's been the first person to be so direct about it. I don't appreciate it. "I'm more than my hair. My life has gone through a lot of changes this past year. I want to be known for my accomplishments as a designer and as a mother. I want people to see me for me, not for the colors on my head."

Chris is taken aback, and I don't even care if I come off as a witch. It empowers me to say it. And I actually mean it.

It seems to take forever to get through the individual interviews with Michele, Weyler, and me. I can't wait for these people to leave so we can sit Michele down and grill her about her intentions. Once they do, man, do we let her have it.

"What did you do?"

"What were you thinking?"

"Why did you do this?"

"What were you thinking?"

Michele holds up her hands as if warding off an attacker, which I guess we are. "Guys, simmer down. I, like, totally thought you'd be stoked. I mean, I couldn't have gotten this opportunity without your help, and I know your work, and if I can't have my friends along for the ride, then what's the point?"

I feel like a jerk. A big, fat, ginormous jerk. It's a great gesture, but pretty presumptuous. Like proposing on a jumbotron. So, yeah, totally something Michele would do.

"Of course, you're right. I'm so sorry, Michele. This whole thing is ... I can't even process it right now." I get up and give her a hug. Weyler expresses a similar sentiment, and we all stand there clinging to each other like fools. There may even be a tear shed. I won't admit who shed it.

I can't wait to tell my mom and Fleur the news. Me—my clothes—are going to be in Cleo's. It's the biggest anchor store in the mall. And I'll be there! It also means I'm going to have my work cut out for me, no pun intended. Michele is emailing us a list of items she wants us to design and pattern and prototype for her final approval.

And what's Tony going to think? Did he know? I'll bet he did. Frankly, I'm surprised Michele was able to keep this from Weyler and me to begin with. With Michele and Tony living together, and Lincoln being Tony's best friend and Michele's boyfriend, there's no way Tony could have *not* known. Part of me wants to be upset with him for keeping this from me. Let's face it, I'm grasping at straws to find the negatives here so I can figure out a reason (other than the obvious, which haven't changed one iota) why I shouldn't be with Tony.

My mind is abuzz, and I walk right by the hotel. I find myself blocks away, totally unsure of where I am. I have to pull out my phone and check the address of the hotel, disoriented. I see a text from Tony, telling me not to plan anything for tonight. I hope that's okay with Fleur. Fleur! I totally forgot that I have to tell Fleur and Mom what happened today. Glancing around, I'm finally able to catch my bearings and walk back as fast as my slouchy boots and leather pants will allow.

The elevator takes forever, and if I were more physically fit, I might even consider running up the stairs to the eighteenth floor. Yeah, no matter what my news, that's not a possibility. My hands are shaking so that I fumble with the stupid card key. Why do these things always seem to foil me? By the time I get the door open, I'm jumping up and down, barely able to contain myself.

"I'm going to be in Cleo's! I'm gonna be in Cleo's!"

"Oh, Mom, I'm all shopped out. I don't want to go shopping tonight." Fleur flops back dramatically on the bed. Where does she get this stuff from?

"No, my clothes—my designs are going to be sold in Cleo's!"

Mom starts jumping up and down with me. "Oh, my God! Kira, that's ... that's fantastic! How? Why? Does this have something to do Michele? Is that why you had to come here?"

I try to perch on the edge of the bed but end up pacing around the room while I recount the story of the "Where Are They Now?" show with Michele's big surprise.

"So, one minute, I'm trying not to cry because Michele is now living my dream, and the next I'm literally falling off my chair at her announcement."

"You fell off the chair?" Mom's got that expression on her face where I can tell she's trying not to laugh. I recognize it, because I often make the same face while dealing with Fleur.

"Yup. On camera. I'm pretty sure they're not going to edit that out either. Especially not after I got snippy with the producer."

"Why did you get snippy?"

"He was giving me sh ... crap," I glance over at Fleur. She's totally paying attention, and I know she would have jumped all over that. "He was giving me crap about coloring my hair brown. He actually said, 'why would you get rid of the only thing you're known for' and that sort of stuff."

"Am I the only one in the world who thinks you look better like this?"

"Probably. Well, not really. Tony said he likes it this way too."

"We'll get back to the Tony thing in a minute. Tell me more about the collection."

I fill her in about how Michele decided to split her collection into three distinct, yet coordinating, styles. The collection will be about twenty pieces total, with Weyler and me each designing five pieces. We're going to be working from the same fabrics and have to collaborate to make sure that my pants can be paired with Weyler's top and Michele's jacket, etc. It'll be a totally unique collection told from three perspectives. It's such an innovative idea. I can't wait to get started.

"That's such a genius move. I wonder if it was all Michele's idea to bring you in or if she was advised to do it?"

"I dunno. I hadn't thought about that yet. It doesn't matter. All that matters is that she did. And this is going to be so much fun."

"How will you do this? Will you have to come back here?" Mom looks at Fleur, who's now sitting on the floor coloring.

"Probably. We're going to share design ideas online of course. Michele will be picking the fabrics. I can request something and give her suggestions, but she'll actually be getting them all. Once we make our pieces, we're going to have to get together to work on them in person and as a team."

"How do you think she'll do?" Mom nods toward Fleur.

"I hope I can make her see that it's okay for me to leave and that I'll always come back. We'll figure it out."

"This sounds fantastic. But onto the good stuff. What's going on with you and Tony?"

Chapter 30

"I don't mean to be a girl, but what should I wear?"

"Aren't you a girl? I mean, I thought I verified fully, but maybe I need to examine you again?"

I giggle. Cripes, I'm thirty-five years old, and he's got me giggling like a schoolgirl. "I'd like that, but you know what I mean. I need a clue about what to wear tonight, since you won't tell me anything about it. I do have a somewhat limited wardrobe at hand, but I can make something work, as long as we're not going ultra-formal." Even as I speak, I know that's not it. Tony, although he looks dashing in a suit, is much more laid back.

"Not super casual. Whatever you wear should be okay."

That doesn't help tons. We disconnect, and I finish getting ready. I've got a gray asymmetrical jersey knit dress with black embellishments that I designed for my *Made for Me* audition. It works with my knee-high black boots. I swear, half of my luggage space is occupied by shoes. Next time I pack for a trip, I need to think this through better.

I've twisted my hair up on top of my head, but long pieces keep escaping. I decide I'm going to rock the messy updo, and I'm finishing my makeup when Tony knocks on the hotel room door.

Mom answers it. Fleur looks at him and says, "You again? I don't want more pizza. It took too long."

"Fleur!" I don't know where this rudeness has come from. I'm definitely seeing changes in her behavior that are not necessarily for the best. "Tony is my friend. I don't like you being rude to my friend."

"But Grammy said we were getting food delivered to our room. I want to do that. I don't want to go out."

"You're not going out. I'm going out with Tony. You still get room service."

That answer seems to appease her. I think she's had her little legs walked off her in the past two days, and her fatigue is showing. Plus, I want her well rested for tomorrow, so I think it's a good thing they're staying in. I give her a hug and a kiss, and she doesn't protest that I'm leaving. She sort of ignores Tony, which I'm okay with for right now. I don't need her becoming overly attached when I don't know what's going to happen.

Of course, I don't need to become overly attached either, but as we stand close in the elevator, our shoulders almost touching, I have a sinking feeling it may be too late.

"Are we eating? I'm hungry." He needs to know that I like my food. I don't want him thinking I'm going to change who I am for him. Plus, I can't stand the tension. I keep thinking about yesterday and how I'd like nothing more than to do that again.

"You don't like to be surprised, do you?"

"Other than today, the surprises in my life recently haven't been fabulous."

"Fair point. We're going to dinner at the Bowery Meat Company. I think you'll like this place. Last time I was there, I had the most amazing meal of my life."

"What was it?"

"Duck lasagna."

The description alone makes me wrinkle my nose. "Duck lasagna? That sounds horrible." If the name of the place is Bowery Meat Company, why would he get duck? I would bet the steaks are fantastic.

"Oh, no, I kid you not; it was amazing. It's a serving for two."

The sinking feeling is back. This is his date place. It's where he takes ladies to make a move. Well, I guess he already made his move on me, so maybe this is the follow up place, and then what? Does he pull out all the stops, send flowers, and then disappear? I think that's called ghosting nowadays. I call it getting the shaft. The last guy I dated before Stan did that—sent me a dozen roses after we slept together and then fell off the face of the earth.

"Let me guess. You took a girl here. This is your date place."

He looks at me and matter of factly says, "Yes."

"Yes to which?" We're walking side by side down Bowery. I feel myself drift, putting space in between us.

"Yes, I took a girl there, and yes, it's my date place. It's fairly close to where I live, and I know it's a good meal. I don't always know it's going to be a good date, so at least I can get some good food, if you know what I mean. I mean, there's nothing worse than having a sucky date, and then overpriced, bad food to boot."

He has a point. I think about the disastrous date with Ted. Good food could have made the evening slightly better. Not much, but anything would have helped. Tony continues. "Once, I let this girl pick the restaurant. She found this place in Brooklyn where you sit at a counter and watch them cook your meal. Frankly, if I want to watch someone cook, I can go watch my mom, but whatever. She seemed into the *experience* of it. So we went. It was over three hundred bucks *per person*. And, since it was a date, she expected me to pay. The whole night, including Lyfts and everything, was over eight hundred bucks. I mean, she was okay, but the assumption that I would drop that kind of money in one night was a huge turn off."

I've stopped walking. "Three hundred dollars a person?"

"Yep."

"I'll watch your mom cook for free any day over that. I know things are expensive in New York, but that's ridiculous."

"It is a three-star Michelin, so you get what you pay for."

"I don't know what that means. Aren't Michelins tires, and I'm not impressed by a restaurant with only three stars?"

"Michelin is some super fancy rating system, and three stars is the best. It's supposed to mean the food is exceptional and worth a detour."

"Is that code for it's worth a month's rent?"

"If my rent were only eight hundred a month, I'd be stoked, but yeah, pretty much."

I have a much better appreciation for finances now that I'm on my own. I've been budgeting for a place, saving up first and last months' rent and figuring out what utilities will cost. I can't even imagine what Tony must pay in rent, even split three ways. There is no way I'd ever in this lifetime be able to afford living here. Nor would I want to. The prices on basic things are so over inflated I'd have to work just to survive, and even then I'm not sure I'd make it.

"We're here." Tony stops and begins to open the door, but the doorman takes care of it from the inside. We're shown to a high-top table nestled up against a wall of shelves displaying wine bottles.

I'm supposed to be looking at the menu, but I find myself looking at Tony instead. There's not a wrinkle on his face. Or anywhere else on his body, as I had the pleasure of finding out. He's wearing a white shirt which shows off his light olive complexion perfectly. In the past I'd been a sucker for blue eyes, but I feel like I could get lost in his brown eyes forever. I've always hated my plain brown eyes, but for the first time, it strikes me how attractive brown eyes can be. Maybe it's because they belong to him.

"What looks good to you?" he asks without looking up.

"You."

Please tell me I did not really just say that.

The wicked grin that spreads across my face tells me I did. Do you think he'll notice if I dive under the table?

"Well, thank you very much. You look especially appetizing yourself tonight, if I do say so. That dress makes your ass look great."

"Thanks. This was one of my audition pieces for the show."

"No wonder you made it. I mean, I know absolutely nothing about fashion, but you look great. You always do though. But what do you want to get from the menu? You know, for food."

I look down again. "Um, how about the charcuterie to start with, and do you want to split something, or what were you thinking?"

"What's on the charcuterie? It says 'chef's choice.'"

"I have no idea, I just like saying charcuterie."

He winks at me. "Then I'll let you order it. And we can do one of the dinners for two, if you want. What are you in the mood for?"

The chef brings over a selection of meat and cheese to pick for our charcuterie. (Okay, I'm done saying it.)

We decide on the chateaubriand (also fun to say). I order a porter, and he orders a Scotch. I noticed in Europe that he drank Scotch. I thought he was trying to be fancy.

"Scotch? Aren't you a little young for that? That's an old man drink."

He frowns slightly. "You're a little hung up on my age, aren't you? How come?"

While I certainly am hung up on it, I didn't think I'd made it that obvious. Apparently I have. "You're young. I'm a lot older than you. I'm at a totally different stage in life."

"How's that? We're both adults. What else is there?"

"You're just out of school. You're a guy. This is the time in your life when you party and sow your oats and find yourself. I've found myself already."

"Have you though?" I catch a hint of defensiveness in his tone, so I match it with my own.

"What is that supposed to mean?"

"What's up with the hair?"

"Didn't we already discuss this?"

"Yes, but answer me. Is this really you? All brown and suburban soccer mom."

"That's who I am. Obviously. I might even buy a minivan."

"I rest my case."

"Huh?" I take a long sip of my beer. This is not how I saw this night going. Not at all.

"The age thing doesn't matter." Before he can finish, our food arrives. We pass a few blissful minutes of silence devouring the most delicate and delectable piece of meat I've ever encountered.

Unable to let that comment lie, I finally ask, "What's that supposed to mean, that age doesn't matter?"

He swallows the bite he's been working on. Nice to see that he doesn't talk with his mouth full. "You haven't found yourself. You're no more likely to drive a minivan than I am to dye my hair purple. It's not you, and you don't even know who you are."

"And I suppose you do?"

"I have a pretty good idea of who you are. I'm also fairly confident in myself and what I want in life."

"Oh really?" I know I'm being sort of a jerk, but he is too. I can't believe he thinks I don't know who I am or what I want.

"Kira, tell me what you want in life. What's important to you?"

That's easy. "My daughter. She's my life. She is the only thing that matters to me."

I see him swallow hard. "The only thing?"

"Yes. My career is a distant second. The only reason it does is that I need my career to build a safe and secure life for Fleur."

"Why are you doing this?"

"Doing what?" I feel my chin sticking out a bit.

"Picking a fight when there's no fight to be had. Pushing me away. Denying that we can be good together."

Even though this is some of the best food I've ever had, I suddenly have no more appetite. Pushing my plate away, I look at Tony squarely. "You see, that's where the difference in maturity comes into play. From the beginning, I've understood that this—whatever—between us could never work. You've never gotten that. We're at different stages in our lives. My first and only priority is my daughter, and I know you can't accept that. Not to mention the fact that we live nowhere near each other. I don't have the time or energy to do the long-distance thing, especially when there's really no chance of it going anywhere. Why bother?"

He throws his napkin down. "Is this how you've always felt? Then why bother? Why yesterday?"

I know I should admit that yesterday happened because I wasn't strong enough to say no to my desires and impulses, even though I should have.

Yesterday was because I wanted it. I wanted him. And I still do, but I know I can't have him. It's better to be proactive and protect myself. I can't go through heartbreak twice in a year. I'm not that strong. This has to end here and now.

Chapter 31

"I can't believe we're having this conversation again, but you need to snap out of it." Mom leans and whispers in my ear. Fleur fell asleep right after takeoff, clutching the prized American Girl doll that she picked out yesterday.

"Leave me alone, Mom. I don't want to talk about it."

"What happened at least? You came back from dinner as ugly as sin and have barely pulled that scowl off your face. Even yesterday, when Fleur was having the greatest day of her life, you were on the verge of ruining it for her all day."

"I'm trying, Mom. That's all I can say is that I'm trying."

"If you tried as hard with Tony as you did to cover up your mood, maybe you wouldn't be in this mood in the first place."

"Are you saying this is my fault? Is it my fault Stan left too? Am I such a terrible person that no one can stand to be with me?"

"What happened with Tony?"

"I realized he's not the right person for me."

"Why not? He seems great."

"Well, on the surface, sure. But there's too much I can't get past. I mean, he said my hair is terrible."

"He actually said that to you? Even if he was thinking it, I can't believe he had the gall to say that out loud."

"Well, he didn't say that, exactly. It was more like I didn't know who I was, and that the brown hair isn't me, any more than driving a minivan is."

"Kira, that's true."

"Wait, I thought you've been waiting for years for my hair to be normal. What are you saying?"

"I'm saying that going from My Little Pony hair to mom-brown with sensible highlights isn't you either. What are you trying to prove?"

"You know I did it because the other moms—and dads—were talking about me." The stewardess passes by and collects our trash. We should be landing soon. Thank goodness, because I'm not loving being trapped in this seat next to my mom with nowhere to go. She's got me.

"When has that ever mattered to you? I mean, I thought most of the reason you colored your hair is so people notice you."

"Well, yes, I liked that people saw me because of my hair. And that was when it didn't impact Fleur. I've got to think about her now."

"Like you haven't been thinking about her for the last five years? You didn't mind when she was in preschool. Or when we're out for ice cream and someone comes up and asks you questions about your hair. Or when you went on national TV with your hair looking like that. You're using Fleur as an excuse because you're afraid."

Her words punch me in the gut and I know she's right. I manage not to admit anything as we start our descent, and Fleur wakes up crying that her ears hurt.

In the deep of the night, alone—of course alone—in my bed, I say what I can't admit in the light of day. I don't know how to do this. I don't know how to put myself in a place where I'm going to get hurt again. I wasn't enough for Stan, so odds are good, that since I'm still me, I'm not good enough for anyone else.

Especially Tony. If he were ten years older and six hundred miles closer, maybe it could work. But those are two things we can't change, so they become the deal breakers. Not to mention that he'd undoubtedly find someone better than me. Like Stan did. Better to break things off before I get really attached. I know how much this is hurting me now. I can't imagine how badly I'd feel if there'd been more intimacy, more getting to know each other. More family. More laughter. More love.

I know I'm not in love with him, not yet. But any fool could see that's where it was heading—at least on my end. I still don't understand what he saw in me. From the first time we met, when I traveled with Michele to the city when we were finishing the show, he's definitely shown an interest. Perhaps it was my fault, because when he flirted with me, I flirted back. After all, I was married at the time, so it seemed harmless. If I'd only had an inkling of where my life was headed, I would have shut it down before it could begin.

I wonder when he's going to come out here again. How often does he come to Columbus anyway? Was that one time a fluke? Or is it regular? No, I have to stop thinking this way. Even if there were a way to work out the distance thing, it doesn't change any of the other stuff.

And as much as I'd like to blame him, we all know that I'm the one who's not ready to be in a relationship.

Wow, I'm not ready. I'm almost thirty-six years old and I can't handle a relationship. Maybe I'm not as mature as I'd thought.

I have reasons. I have baggage. But what I don't have is an excuse for being a colossal ass to Tony. I text him as much.

I shouldn't be surprised that he doesn't answer. It is about two in the morning after all. And, if the shoe were on the other foot, I don't know that I'd be jumping to reply. I'd want to make him suffer a little bit. Or a lot bit.

The sleepless night does little for my mood the next day, especially considering I have to go into work. I'm under a gag order from the show until the special airs, so I can't even share the good news with my co-workers. I'm not sure what I'm going to tell them about my trip to New York. I know they're going to want something though.

So I tell them about Tony. And then I endure four hours of ribbing about how could I have been so mean and stupid. I don't have any answers, because I still don't know. I mean I do know, but I'm not going to admit that I'm a hot mess in the middle of House of Crafts.

Folding bolts upon bolts of fabric, Morris asks, "If he wasn't good enough, will anyone ever be?"

I sort of wish someone—anyone—would take my side in this. "You know, it's only been like two days, but I sort of see Tony as harder to get over than Stan in some ways. Stan was there, like a comfortable pair of jeans that I wore a few times a week. He was always gone, and when he was on the road, I didn't even hear from him. Now I know why, but at the time, it was almost like we had two separate lives going on. I think that's why the distance thing freaks me out so much. Tony though—talk about a crush. I haven't felt like this since I was probably a teenager. And now, I'm crushed."

"Are you going to keep dating though?"

"Nah. I'm good. My mom never needed to. I probably don't either."

I pretend to ignore Morris wrinkling his nose in distaste. I put the last bolt on the stack and begin pulling supplies I'm going to need for my first class next week. I don't want to do this anymore.

But I can't quit now. Michele's going to be calling tonight with details about the collection, but I don't think that's going to pay the bills. At least not for a long while. Maybe someday I can make my living as a clothing designer, but that day isn't today.

I have to avoid Marty the Manager at work because I never asked Michele if she'd come make an appearance here. I'm sure she'd do it, but I know Marty's looking for an answer now. And we all know, the one thing I don't have right now is answers.

My shift seems interminably long. Mom's picking me up, because her car is in the shop, and she had some appointments today. I don't care that she took my car, as long as we don't have to talk on the way home. Still no answer from Tony.

I flop into the front seat, much like the moody teenager I once was. The weather outside is gray and rainy, which matches my mood perfectly. I was probably not the most pleasant at work today, and that's fine with me. We're headed to school to pick up Fleur, and I'll have to be chipper then. Well, if not chipper, at least not as sullen. I can't let her know that I'm miserable.

"Wait, where are you going? School's the other way."

Mom doesn't say anything.

"Mom! Where are you going? We have to get Fleur."

"I know. I'm dropping you off first."

"Wait, what? Where?"

"I called your hairdresser and made you an appointment. We're getting that taken care of once and for all."

"What does my hair have to do with any of it?"

Mom pulls up at the salon and pushes the stick into park, perhaps a little more forcefully than needed. "Do I have to spell it out for you?"

I have no idea where she's going with this. "Apparently."

"I can't believe I'm saying this, but you need to do something. You're moody and miserable and making terrible choices. And it all started with you going back to your natural color. Who cares what other people think? You know who you are. You know what you want. Stop focusing on what you've lost, and what you could lose. Grab the bull by the horns and seize the day."

"Mom, you're mixing your clichés again."

"You know what I mean. Go in there and tell Emay to fix this. Do what you have to do to make you feel like you again."

"I thought you hated my hair."

"I did, but at least it was you. And you felt good about yourself. You need that again."

"There's not a lot to feel good about these days, Mom."

"Well, fix the mess on your head, and then fix everything else. There's only not a solution if you don't want there to be."

Seriously, when did my mom get so smart?

Chapter 32

"How did you mess this up so badly? He's miserable."

"Michele, I don't want to talk about Tony with you."

"Why not?" Even though we're on the phone, I'm fairly confident that she's impatiently tapping her toes.

"Because we're in business together, and he's your roommate and cousin. Those things don't mix, and I don't want to jeopardize our business relationship and friendship."

"But he's so mean right now."

"Yes, and I take responsibility and now we're changing topics. We need to focus on the collection."

This phone call has been delayed several days due to one reason or another. I've continued working hard on the Etsy orders as we've got to get those wrapped up before we start the new collection. I can't design anything anyway until I get the instructions from Michele and know what she needs me to do. If the show hadn't been taped and promos already aired, I'd be skeptical that this deal would fall through imminently.

"I'm looking at fabrics and trying to figure out what'll be hot for next fall. We need to be super on."

"Well, we're not striving to be passé before we even release."

"So, I'm thinking if you do two tops, one pant, a skirt, and a dress, and Weyler can do the same. What do you think?"

"Sounds good. We need to share design ideas so we're all on the same page."

"Yeah. Are you going to be able to come to New York again?"

Sighing, I don't want to answer. "You know that's going to be difficult. Do I really have to?"

"It would be better once we start mocking things up. I won't make you see Tony."

"It's not Tony." It partly is. If I never have to go to New York again, it's fine with me. "I can't leave Fleur."

"Okay, well, I don't have kids, and I'm going to go out on a limb here. I understand your point about leaving. It's totally valid. But if you don't leave her ever, how is she ever going to leave? Isn't it going to make her clingy and stuff? Like, won't it make her latch onto someone, even if he's not the right guy for her?"

My first instinct is to snap at Michele. She doesn't have kids. Frankly, I can't imagine her with kids. What right does she have to make such judgments? Except I can't say any of this to her, because deep down, I know she's right. Fleur's faith in people has been shaken. Just as mine has. We're trying to figure it out. However, that might mean making mistakes along the way. Heavens knows I'm making mistakes left and right. I only hope that my mistakes aren't doing irrevocable damage to Fleur. I have a feeling the damage is already done when it comes to me.

While these thoughts are running through my head, Michele must take my silence for agreement. "I mean, I understand why you couldn't leave Fleur to come here. We all understood. Heck, it's why Tony bought the tickets for your mom and Fleur. He knew how important it would be to your career to be here, and he didn't want you to sacrifice that, even though you totally would have, to—"

"STOP!" I jump to my feet and stare at my phone, as if looking at it will help make sense of what she just said.

"What?"

"Ooops, I wasn't supposed to say that."

"What weren't you supposed to say? That Tony bought my mom and Fleur's tickets?"

"Yeah. He made me promise not to tell you. He's going to kill me."

Suddenly my knees feel weak. It's been a week since I saw him or even talked to him, since he won't answer my texts. Again. The longest week.

"I messed this up." My voice cracks and comes out as a croak.

"Yeah, you did. I don't get what your problem is. Tony's a great guy. You know he'd be good to Fleur. Family's the most important thing to him. He'd do anything for his family."

"I couldn't see it. I was too stuck in my own thing. My own mess. I couldn't see outside of myself. I got too hung up on the logistics and didn't even try to see if it could work."

"You blew it. You're never going to find anyone like him again."

"I don't think I will."

I know Michele's right. Of course she's right. I've messed this up right from the beginning. If I could go back—all the way back to that night in Montabago—I'd do it all differently. When he laughed at my Spanx, I'd realize how ridiculous it looked and laugh with him. When he had dinner here at the house, I wouldn't have kissed him to make Stan jealous. I'd have kissed him because his lips are delicious, and I can't help but press my body into his. And when he took me out to a romantic dinner, I'd have told him how scared I was, but that I thought we could get through it together.

If ifs and ands were pots and pans, a herd of elephants couldn't piss them full, and if ifs and buts were candy and nuts, it would be Christmas every day.

I can't go back, and it's not like this is a movie where I can hop on a plane and make some romantic gesture to make it all right. This is real life, and sometimes, people mess up, and it doesn't all work out in the end.

Stan moved on from me, and there's nothing I could do about it. But this is all me. I messed this up, and it's going to take me a while to swallow that bitter pill.

Chapter 33

"Mom, I can't do this. I'm going to be sick."

"No, you're not. You're going to be fine. We'll be at the hotel waiting for you."

"Mom, I can't ..."

"Get out of the car before I throw you out."

"You wouldn't do that to me!"

"Wanna make a bet?"

I step out of the car and start up the driveway. Festive lights in paper bags line the path to the house. The windows of the house are fogged, indicating the presence of warm bodies on a cold night.

I can't believe Mom is making me do this. Well, I can, because she absolutely, positively believes it's the right thing to do. I don't necessarily agree with her, especially considering the timing.

If I were walking up the driveway any slower, I'd be going backwards. I hear footsteps behind me and try to pretend that I'm not literally dragging my feet.

"Kira? Hey, I didn't know you were in town. Merry Christmas!"

"Merry Christmas Christine. Hi Patrick."

I walk up the driveway with the happy couple, mere weeks away from their wedding. Michele's been a little distracted with work, so I feel badly that Christine's had to put her wedding together by herself. She is a professional wedding planner, and Michele designed her dress months ago, but there are still lots of details to be dealt with.

"How are the wedding plans going?"

"Oh you know. We're going crazy."

Patrick nudges her. "Speak for yourself. You're going crazy. I'm fine."

We reach the front door. The storm door is closed but the inner door is open. I extend my hand to ring the bell.

"Oh, no, you don't have to do that. You can just go in." Christine pulls the door open. Patrick takes it from her and holds it so we can both pass through.

"Merry Christmas!" "Merry Christmas!" Voices call out in greeting. Christine and Patrick are whispering in each other's ears, the look on their faces sheer bliss. Makes me want to vomit.

Christine catches me looking at them, and a warm smile spreads across her face. "I was reminding Patrick that one year ago, I was invited to be here, but I couldn't face the holiday. I'd had a stressful year and planned to spend the night at home, stuffing my face. I ran to Wal-Mart, and that's where Patrick and I finally connected. So, this is sort of our anniversary."

"Awwww, that's so sweet." So sweet. Sickeningly sweet. I may barf. Seriously. My stomach is a mess, and I can't believe I'm doing this. This is even riskier than trying out for some stupid TV show. This is my whole life, and it's probably going to be played out in the next five minutes. Here goes nothing.

"Kira! How nice to see you! Michele forgot to tell me you were coming. No matter. I'm so glad you're here!" Mrs. Nowakowski pulls me into a tight hug. I'd spent six weeks holed up here working with Michele on her final designs for the contest. I love Michele's family. I really do. They're what a big, loud family should be. I also love that she simply assumes Michele forgot to tell her, not that I showed up uninvited. Not actually uninvited, because Mrs. Nowakowski did tell me the door was always open.

"You did say I was welcome anytime. I hope it's okay I'm here."

"Of course, dear. Michele and Lincoln aren't here yet, though I expect them any time. Lynn and Larry are here with the baby, not that she'll let anyone hold him. Ridiculous, really. It's how a baby builds his immune system. But it's so good to have a little one in the family again. Maybe Michele and Lincoln will get their acts together and get married quickly, so I can be a grandmother again before I die. I'm not getting any younger, you know."

I'm used to the guilt trip Michele's mom likes to give, and I'm thankful my own mom doesn't do that. There's so much pressure in this family to get married and have babies. I don't have to guess what their feelings on divorce are.

As I mill through the house, I've got to wonder who knows what about Tony and me. They're a tight family, but on the other hand, I can't see him giving details of his sex life to his aunt Rosalie. The glare I get from his sister, Alessandra, though, tells me she, at least, knows something. Awesome. Nothing like having a twenty-year-old enemy. She doesn't have the wisdom or maturity to understand what I'm going through, or even what I've been through this year. Gosh, it's been one hell of a rollercoaster. I finally make it through the throngs of people to the back living room where the men are camped out.

And there he is, sitting comfortably on the quilt-covered sofa, sandwiched between Lynn's husband, Larry, and Michele's brother John. When he sees me, his hand freezes midway to bringing his Scotch and soda to his mouth. Lucky for me, the other men in the room are too oblivious to notice this momentous occasion and continue their discussions about I-don't-even-know-what. I can't hear anything.

I can, however smell, and the smell of fish is overwhelming. The women are in the kitchen, plating up the last of the serving dishes. It smells like an aquarium in here. Is it me, or is it getting hot? I fan my face and fight back the wave of nausea washing over me. I've got to get out of here before I make a royal embarrassment of myself.

I turn and promptly run into someone. I stumble a bit and ask in a frantic voice where the bathroom is. I'm so disoriented that I don't remember, even though I spent weeks in this house last spring. I feel like I'm a running back pushing my way through the Pittsburgh Steelers defensive line, all the while clamping my lips together in hopes I don't spew everywhere. Nothing ruins a good party faster than vomit.

I make it in time to relieve my stomach of its meager contents. Wiping my face, I look up to see Tony standing in the doorway. He does not look happy to see me. Can't say I blame him.

"So, yeah. This." I flush the toilet and sit back against the wall, not straying far in case another wave hits.

"Are you sick?"

"Periodically throughout the day."

"Why are you sick?"

He's slowly putting two and two together, but I can see that he doesn't want to know the answer. He steps fully into the bathroom and shuts the door behind him. Believe me, I don't want this answer either. Just when I thought I couldn't screw things up any more, I go and do. Damn my body for betraying me.

"I'm sorry. You wouldn't answer my texts, and this isn't really something I want to say in a text anyway." Gingerly, I stand up and head to the sink. I wash my hands and pull some toothpaste out of the medicine cabinet. I use my finger to brush my teeth and get the horrible taste out of my mouth. The mint helps calm my stomach for a minute, allowing me to finally turn and face Tony.

"I'm sorry," I repeat. I really am. "I had to tell you. I understand if you still want nothing to do with me. I'm a hot mess. I get it. I've messed everything up. It's all me. I ..." I drop my hands down, my shoulders sagging. I can't meet his eyes. "I'm sorry."

I don't want him to see me cry. I have enough nights to cry myself to sleep. I will forever be reminded of my foolishness, my hastiness, my stubbornness.

Finally, Tony speaks. "Kira, what are you saying?"

"I'm an idiot."

"I know that. What else are you saying?"

Maybe he's not as sharp as I thought. "Tony, I'm pregnant."

He sucks air in. I know what it's like trying to breathe and not quite managing it. I had the same experience in my bathroom three weeks ago. "Michele's couch."

"Are you sure?"

"Um, yeah because we used something the other time. And it's not like there's been anyone else."

"No, I meant are you sure you're pregnant?"

I let out a small laugh. "Quite sure. Either that or I have an odd virus that makes me puke, makes my boobs sore, and takes away my period."

I look him square in the eye. His face has gone a bit pale, and for a minute I'm worried he's going to pass out. He sags against the door a bit.

"Look, Tony, I'm not going to ask you for anything. It's not your fault. Well, it sort of is, but I'm not going to punish you because I was careless. I just wanted you to know. So, um, if you let me by, I'll go now."

Instead of moving, Tony begins banging his head on the door. Slowly at first but with enough force to make me wince at every strike.

"Dammit, Kira, when are you going to stop jumping to conclusions? Haven't you done that enough?"

"Jumping to conclusions is about the only form of exercise I get." The look on his face tells me it's not time for a joke. Okey-dokey.

He continues, working himself up into a good rant. "Why would you come here and tell me this if you don't want me involved? What do you think of me exactly? If I'm such a horrible person, why did you even bother with me? Don't you know me at all?"

"I do know you're good and loving and loyal."

"Then why would you think I wouldn't be there for you?"

"I don't want to force this on you. It wasn't your choice."

"I'm guessing it wasn't yours either. And if I remember correctly, there were two of us there. So, there will be two of us."

His words take my breath away.

"Really?"

"Really."

"But I've messed everything up. I've pushed you away."

"And I've let myself be pushed away."

"You're still too young."

"And you're still too hung up on age. When will you realize that age ain't nothin' but a number?"

"When you realize that I'm using it as an excuse to protect myself."

"And when will you realize you don't need protecting from me but *by* me?"

"Can I hug you now?"

"Only if you don't throw up on me."

"I make no promises."

Chapter 34

A knock on the door interrupts our perfect moment, if a bathroom can be the setting for a perfect moment.

"I guess we'd better go and tell the family." Tony's still got his arm around me. I don't want him to ever take it away.

"Now? We've got to tell the family now?"

"Everyone's together. Seems as good a time as any."

"Are your parents going to be upset?"

"Nah, they're going to be happy. They get to be grandparents. Mom can keep up with Aunt Phyllis in that department."

"Right, who doesn't love babies?"

Large, traditional Catholic families when the baby is conceived out of wedlock, that's who. I express my concern, but Tony doesn't share it.

"Nah, it'll be great."

"I'm not ready yet. It's still early. What if something happens?"

"Fine, we'll keep it for ourselves tonight, but you know how we are with secrets in this family."

"I know. Terrible."

"So I won't make any promises."

We exit the bathroom and promptly receive a dirty look from Alessandra. "Really, guys? That's disgusting. You don't do that at a family member's place. Gross."

Her words hit a bit too close to home, and we both start laughing. Tony whispers in my ear, "Oh, if she only had any idea."

"If Michele had any idea."

This sends us into more laughter, and Tony comfortably slips his hand into mine as we walk back into the front room. Antonia and Carmalina are there with Michele's sister-in-law, Jordan, who can be pretty nasty, if I remember correctly.

"You're with *her*?" Yup, Jordan is pretty nasty. "At least her hair looks normal now."

No one else in the room can speak for a minute. Tony looks at my hair and says, "I sort of miss the color."

I turn my back to him and lift up the top of the back of my hair. Hidden about halfway down is a rainbow. I can wear my hair down and go incognito, or put the top of my hair up to show the vibrant strip of colors.

"That's perfect. It's you."

"You were right. About so many things. But this too." I turn back to face him and find I can't tear my gaze away. Nor do I want to.

Michele's mom comes out. "As soon as Michele and Lincoln get here, we're going to eat."

Mike, Michele's dad, walks up behind her. "We're not waiting. Too bad if they're late. It's Michele—she's always late. Let's eat!"

Tony and I fall in line between his aunt Rosalie and uncle Mario. With this many people, there's no choice but to serve the meal buffet style. That makes it tricky, considering there's soup (a lobster bisque, if I'm not mistaken), salad (although Tony informs me it's an antipasto), and all the other ... fish. Everything on the buffet is fish. No wonder the house smells like this. It's not me and my pregnancy hormones. There's seafood dish after seafood dish after seafood dish. I wonder if anyone will notice if I only eat bread?

As discreetly as possible, I say to Tony, "It's all seafood."

"Yeah, it's the seven fishes. We do this every Christmas Eve."

"I can't eat fish."

"Oh because of ..." he glances down at my midsection.

"No. I mean, yes. It's not that I'm not supposed to; it's the smell. That's what made me throw up before."

"Okay, well, take what you can. Aunt Phyll usually has a back-up tray of lasagna in the kitchen, in case we run out of food."

I look at the table, absolutely packed with food, and wonder how on earth they could ever run out. "Is there always this much food?"

"On Christmas Eve, yes. We're Italian. We like to eat and then eat some more."

"So I might fit in?"

Tony shuffles behind me, propelling me toward the kitchen. I'm not the only one to dig into the "secret" lasagna. There's a tiny bit of counter space left, and we claim it with our plates. Tony has so much food piled on his that I don't know how it doesn't collapse in half.

With the fork midway to his mouth, Tony pauses. "So you really flew all the way here just to tell me? What about Fleur?"

"I haven't told her yet, but Mom knows."

"I mean, how could you leave her on Christmas?"

"Oh, I didn't. They're here too. They're at the hotel."

"Well, call them and tell them to come over! What were you thinking? Why didn't they just come with you?"

"Because I was barging in unannounced as it was. I didn't think it would be cool to bring an entourage. Especially when I thought you might throw me out on my ear."

"Did you really think I'd do that?"

I shrug. "If I were in your shoes, I would have. I've been terrible to you. Truly."

"I haven't always been the best either. Remember Montabago? And when I got all mad because you kissed me to make your ex jealous? I should have been happy you were kissing me."

"True. And you don't let me apologize to you. You simply stopped answering my texts and calls. That makes it hard to make it up to you."

"Yeah, but I make up for it in grand gestures."

"Like paying for my mom and Fleur to come to New York?"

"She told you? I can't believe it!"

"When have you ever known Michele to keep a secret?"

"True. So, she doesn't know the news yet, I take it?"

"No. It's you and my mom. That's it."

"Did you text her yet to come over?" He taps his foot impatiently.

"Fine. I will." I pull my phone out and send her a quick text. She immediately responds that they'll be here soon.

See? This is working out even better than I had any right to hope. I don't know what I expected, but it wasn't this. I lean over and give Tony a quick kiss. He looks a little stunned and pulls back.

"Oh, I'm sorry. Was that not okay? I thought you were okay with me. I get it; you're just okay with the situation. I'm sorry. I won't do it again. I'll contain myself from now on. I'm sure eventually my feelings will go away."

He takes my face in his hands. "I don't want your feelings to go away. Not now, and not eventually. I was surprised because I didn't think you wanted to be with me. I thought it was just about the ... you know what." His voice drops to a hush. People are in and out of the kitchen, and despite the din, he's concerned about being overheard.

"Will we ever not be at cross purposes?" With my shoes on, we're almost the same height. I love being able to stare right into his eyes. God, I could get lost in them. I think I may have already.

"If we start listening to each other instead of letting our own thoughts get in the way."

"How did you get to be so wise in your limited years?"

"I keep telling you, age ain't nothin' but a number, baby."

"Eeew, don't say that. It sounds like some cheap, sleazy pick-up line."

"Is it working?"

Before I can answer, my eardrums are shattered by the high-pitched squealing that only Michele can manage. I swear she's fluent in dolphin. "KIRA! What are you doing here? I can't believe it! You're here! And you ..." she looks from me to Tony to me again. Our close proximity is a dead giveaway. "... you're back together? When did this happen? Why didn't you tell me? Tony, you've been so miserable. Has that all been an act? God, I'm so happy!"

Sometimes, listening to Michele makes me tired.

She's waving her arms about, and something catches my eye. Something large and sparkly that certainly wasn't there the last time I saw her.

"Um, Michele—" I grab her hand as it's flailing. "Is there something you want to tell us?"

She starts jumping up and down, and I swear she's vibrating. The kitchen is becoming more and more packed by the minute, people cramming in to see what all the commotion is about.

"I know! I KNOW!"

She's waving her hand about, the ring catching the light. Lincoln's standing behind her, smiling proudly. He's as in love with her as she is with him, and they're made for each other. He's good for her, a nice logical balance.

"We're getting MARRIED!!!"

There's a round of applause and hugs, the crowd crushing in. I'm pressed into Tony, not that I'm complaining. Christine and Lynn are crushing Michele. I think they're jumping up and down. The whole kitchen feels like a mosh pit.

Uncle Vito comes into the room, carrying a bottle of sambuca, and announces, "A drink for everyone!"

Shot glasses appear out of nowhere, and it boggles the mind that there are enough for everyone. Uncle Vito is busy pouring and passing. Tony's dad hands one to me.

"Um, no thank you."

"Why not? What, are you pregnant or something?"

I never knew a room full of boisterous Italians could go quiet so quickly.

Chapter 35

"You know how to kill a party, don't you?"

I know Tony's teasing me, but I don't find him funny. Not in the least. The barrage of questions, his mom swooning. Who knew women still swooned? There were some loud voices. I think in this family the voices are almost always loud, but these were even louder. There's definitely a generational divide in regard to the whole out-of-wedlock baby. Alessandra, unexpectedly siding with her elders, took the cake when she called me a 'hag' who was probably lying about paternity. Tony shut her down immediately. I think there are going to be a lot of fences to mend here. We've got time.

We're sitting on the couch in the front living room. It's just Tony, his parents, and me. The rest of the house's inhabitants have been quarantined in the kitchen and the back of the house, including my mom, who arrived just in time to hear the barrage of verbal assault. His parents start up again.

"What are you thinking?"

"How could this be?"

"Didn't we talk about getting girls in trouble?"

"I wouldn't call her a girl. She's the adult here. She obviously seduced him."

"Are you sure it's yours? Did you ever think she's trying to trap you?"

That's where I draw the line.

"Wait just a minute everyone." My voice is a lot louder than I'd like it to be. I'm sure the people in the back of the house appreciate being able to hear what's going on. "There was no trapping. There was no seducing. Well, I mean, obviously there was, but not in the way you mean. Granted, this was not a planned thing, but we're ..."

Tony jumps in. "We're happy about it, and we'll figure it out."

Tony's dad looks at me sternly. "Where do you even live?"

I squirm in my seat, unused to the male authority figure, since mine left before I really needed any discipline. "Um, Columbus, Ohio ... sir."

"So how is this even going to work? Are you just looking to collect a check from Tony, but he never even gets to see his kid?"

My mom bursts into the room. I hope that someone is entertaining Fleur so she doesn't come in and hear this. "That's quite enough. I believe Kira and Tony said they'd figure something out. This is all very new, and we've all had a bit of excitement tonight. Now, instead of vilifying Kira and Tony, why don't you stop for a minute to realize that your family will be gaining both Lincoln and a new baby in the new year?"

Tony leans over. "Your mom is sort of awesome. I may have a crush on her now. You know I have a thing for older women." I elbow him and then settle into his side.

"Yes, my mom is sort of awesome."

"As is her daughter."

"We do have a lot to figure out though."

"Are we going to be able to do anything about it tonight?"

"Probably not, no."

"Then let's enjoy the rest of the evening. I'm sure we're going to have to answer tons of questions."'

I sit up tall. "I've got an idea. How about every time someone asks about us or the baby, we ask Michele a question about weddings?"

"Yeah, Linc and I'll probably head out back and smoke a cigar. It's a tradition. Of course, the first time we did it, it made us both puke."

"Nice. How old were you?"

"Um, maybe about thirteen?"

"Oh, so last year."

Now it's his turn to elbow me. "No, last year, we almost didn't have time. Lincoln had to take Michele home to change clothes. I'm pretty sure that's when he started trying to get in her pants."

"Nice."

"It's been a good year for us. If only all those girls in high school could see us now."

"I might be sick again."

Tony springs up, ready to help, even though he obviously has no idea what he's doing.

"Sit down. I'm fine. I meant about the girls in high school. Which, again, was like last year."

"I hope you're kidding. You've got to get past the age thing. We're in this for the long haul."

"Do you want to be in it for the long haul?"

He pulls me in close, crushing me against his chest. "Even if I hadn't gotten you in trouble, I'd want you for the long haul. Since the moment I met you, I wanted you for the long haul."

"Please don't refer to it as 'getting me in trouble.' It's not 1950. But thank you for not giving up."

"I did, quite a few times. But you wouldn't stay away. Or I couldn't stay away."

"I couldn't. Even though I should have."

He pulls back slightly to look at me. "Why? Why should you have? Doesn't this feel right?"

"When you first expressed interest, I was married, so I didn't think much of it. Then, in Montabago, I'm not sure if you caught onto it, but I wasn't exactly in a good place. I was looking for a meaningless hook up. If it hadn't been you, it would have been some anonymous European stranger. I'm a train wreck. I'm all insecure now, and trust is very difficult."

"You can trust me." He takes both my hands in his. I know he's sincere.

"In my head, I know that. But it's my heart that's been damaged, and she's sort of overriding logic at the moment. I mean, showing up at your family's house on Christmas Eve isn't totally logical."

"Yeah, why did you do that?"

"Do you want the long answer or the short answer?"

"The short answer."

Of course he would say that. Such a guy thing.

"My mom made me."

"Huh. Okay, yeah, I'm going to need more than that."

"I'm messed up and can't think clearly on a good day, add in crazy hormones, and I'm making very poor choices at this point in my life. So, Mom made me. I refused to show up on your doorstep in New York. I thought if there were family around, and, you know, Michele and stuff, it wouldn't seem so odd."

"And you didn't think today was maybe not the best?"

"Well, considering I only told my mom two days ago, this was the best we could do."

"You got a Christmas Eve flight on two days' notice?"

I roll my eyes. "I wish it were that easy. We drove. Do you know about this thing called 'lake-effect snow?' If you don't, let me tell you to avoid the area from Cleveland to Syracuse for all winter months."

"Oh, yeah. It's terrible out there. How long did it take you? I can't believe you drove."

"It was supposed to take nine to ten hours. It took about fourteen. With a five-year-old, a fifty-eight-year-old bladder, and morning sickness. Yesterday blew chunks, both literally and figuratively."

"Yeah, no thanks."

I pull away from him. "But don't you understand? That's what you're signing on for. It's not just about me and the baby. It's Fleur too. And my mom. We're a package deal. And it's a big package. A lot more than you bargained for. So I understand if you're not ready for the package."

As if she knew we were talking about her, Fleur comes running into the room. "There's a kid out there who says Santa's not coming for me because I'm not home. Did you tell Santa we're here? He's coming for me, right?"

There are tears filling her big green eyes. "Of course, baby. Santa knows right where you are. I'm sure he's got it taken care of."

"How do you know?"

"I called the hotline myself and talked to an elf. He knows we're in New York."

Her lower lip is still quivering, but I can tell she wants to believe it. I pull her onto my lap, and she snuggles in. Tony leans over. "Your mom's right. When you become a mom, they tell you how to do all these things. And the last thing your mom would want is for you to have a bad Christmas, so you know it's all set."

She nods, trying to be brave. Poor girl. "Now, go find Gramma. I think we're going to head back to the hotel soon. We want to go to sleep so the big man can come, right?"

She gets up and scampers off. "I've made such a mess of things that she's not even sure Santa will come for her."

Tony looks at me. "What are you going to do?"

"Um, wait until she goes to sleep and then bring everything in from the car."

"Is there even a tree in your room?"

"No, of course not. I'll just pile the gifts by the door."

He jumps up. "Um, go talk to Michele for a bit, but don't leave before I see you again. There's something I've got to do."

And with that, he disappears out the front door. He'd better not be out smoking that cigar right now.

The past few days have been more draining than I'd care to think about. All I want right now is to go to bed.

Chapter 36

I do have to start trusting Tony at some point, so I get up and find Michele, who's still flanked by Christine and Lynn. They pull me into the huddle and start the barrage of questions. At least this time, they're the supportive kind, like "when are you due?" and "are you going to find out?" I've never been one for girlfriends. I was always more of a loner, and then I had Stan. And I didn't need friends because I had my mom. There's something refreshing about being with my own cohort, travelling on our life journeys together. We could make up a sitcom: the new mom, the pregnant girl, the one about to get married, and the newly engaged. Instead of *Sex in the City*, we could be *Sex in the Suburbs*.

Someone hands me a glass of ginger ale and we're able to toast to all the good news. Michele looks at all of us. "So between last year and this, we've had two engagements and one ..." she looks over at me, "and a half babies." She raises her glass to all of us.

"Not to mention a reality show winner, a royal wedding, and a department store contract." Christine holds up her glass to toast Michele.

Lynn holds up her glass. "Here's to lots of practice baby making and to fertility drugs."

"Or not lots of practice, just the right couch in the right studio." I raise my glass.

"Wait—studio? What studio? *MY studio?* Ewwww, that's gross. I'm going to have to burn that thing now."

I can't believe I said that out loud. Oops. Tony's going to kill me when he finds out I told her. "You can't tell Tony I told you. I wasn't supposed to say anything."

"She can't tell me you told her what?" Tony slinks up behind me and puts his arms around my waist, locking his hands comfortably in front of my midsection.

"Um, nothing. Don't worry about it."

He leans forward and rests his chin on my shoulder.

"Where did you take off to anyway? That was quick to smoke a cigar."

"Nah, I didn't do that. We'll do that right before mass. I was talking to my mom and getting everything set. It's good to go."

"Set? What's good to go?" I wish I could turn around and talk to him, but this is pretty comfortable too. I sort of never want to leave his arms.

"For the morning. I got the stuff out of your trunk. Come over to the house. It'll be under the tree."

"But what am I going to tell her when she wakes up and there's nothing there? She's so insecure already—"

"Like her mama?"

"Precisely. She doesn't have a lot of faith to go on right now."

"Trust me, I took care of it. It'll be fine."

"Her mama doesn't have tons of faith either, in case you hadn't noticed." I know he knows it, but I need him to hear it again.

That makes him spin me around so we're facing each other, his hands still around my waist, drawing me into him.

"We're going to have to do something about that." He smiles and kisses me. "You know, faith is something you choose to have."

"I'm trying. I can't just flip my attitude about everything overnight."

"Maybe you should ask Santa to bring you a new one for Christmas?"

"Do you think he can deliver such a tall order on such short notice?"

"Don't tell anyone, but when I was about nine, I discovered that Santa doesn't really exist. When I asked my mom about it, she said he does, that he's the spirit of giving and miracles that the season is about. I can't promise you a miracle, and I can't miraculously change your attitude, but I can promise to do the best I can to give you what you need. If it's space, I'll give you that. If it's support, it's yours. Just let me do for you what I can and be here for you."

What's a girl to say or do when someone says that to her? Other than cry, which of course I start doing. I give Tony a long kiss, way too indecent for all the family to see, and then say, "Yeah, but you're wrong."

"Wrong? What am I wrong about now?"

"That you can't perform miracles. Because I just felt one."

"Are you sure that's not indigestion?"

I give him a little push with my hip and wrinkle my nose in his general direction. "No, it's got to be a miracle, because all of a sudden, I've got a new outlook on life. And you know, what? I don't know anything. I don't know how this is going to play out. I don't know how it's going to work. The only thing I do know is that no matter the age, no matter the distance, no matter what, we're supposed to be together."

"You're just coming to that realization now? I could have told you that the first time I met you."

"Like I said, it's a Christmas miracle."

My mom comes up with Fleur and gives me the look that tells me we need to leave. I can see Fleur is on the edge of a meltdown, and I certainly don't need Tony's family thinking any worse of me. At least not tonight.

Tony's mom appears with our coats. "Kira, I'm so sorry about before. I, um, well, it wasn't what I was expecting to hear tonight."

"You and me both, Mom." Tony's grinning from ear to ear, like I actually made his Christmas rather than ruined it. "I'm gonna drive Kira back to the hotel. I'll be back before it's time to go to mass."

We get in the car and I glance over at him. "I'm so sorry about how I've handled everything. I'm an idiot. You deserve more than me."

"No, I think I deserve you. I'm an idiot a lot of the time too." He can't stop smiling. "And I'm coming back to the hotel, because I have a note to drop off for the morning for Fleur, just so she doesn't freak out. You've got to trust me."

And I do. His smile is virtually illuminating the car. I didn't ruin his night. He's happy about this. He wants to be with me. He wants this baby. He wants to be a part of Fleur's life.

And more important, I want him here for all this. I have to trust that he's not going to tire of me. That he's going to want me, no matter what color my hair. That he's going to be as good a man as I know he is.

And I do. Like a switch has been flipped, without a doubt, I know all this. "Tony, thank you. Thank you for not giving up on me, even when I didn't deserve it."

"You know, I really wish you'd stop being so hard on the woman I love. It's annoying."

"The old me only would have heard that you called me annoying, but the new me, the one with the new attitude, only thinks she heard you say you love me."

"Of course I do. I wouldn't have fought this hard if I didn't."

I barely know what to say to that. I'm quiet for a minute, searching deep within myself.

"Well, I love you too."

"Just remember who said it first."

"I'm sure you won't ever let me forget, but it doesn't matter. All that matters is that we love each other and keep on loving each other."

"That's my plan."

"Good, now we're finally on the same page."

As if with a brand new sketchbook, unmarred by pencil smudges and wrinkled by use, I'm about to open the cover and see what this new life can hold for me. It's my turn for a one-word note.

Ready.

THE END

ACKNOWLEDGMENTS

To my beta crew: Becky Monson, Aven Ellis, Laura Chapman, and Michele Vagianelis. Thank you for talking about my made up people as if they were real.

Karen Pirozzi and Marlene Engle, thank you for your editing talents. I'm trying to learn, but will always need you to keep me on the straight and narrow.

Thank you to Erin Parker for not only giving a great cut and color, but for answering my seemingly random questions about purple hair (and how to un-purple it).

To the Chick Lit Chat HQ and Wenches. You know who you are and what you've done.

My accountability group: Wendy, Becky, and Melissa. I didn't think I could get it done but you all made me do it. I blame you.

To my parents for their unwavering support, and Patrick, Jake, and Sophia. Thanks for putting up with me and writing along side me.

Kathryn R. Biel

ABOUT THE AUTHOR

Telling stories of resilient women, Kathryn Biel hails from Upstate New York and is a wife and mother to two wonderful and energetic kids. In between being Chief Home Officer and Director of Child Development of the Biel household, she works as a school-based physical therapist. She attended Boston University and received her Doctorate in Physical Therapy from The Sage Colleges. After years of writing countless letters of medical necessity for wheelchairs, finding increasingly creative ways to encourage the government and insurance companies to fund her clients' needs, and writing entertaining annual Christmas letters, she decided to take a shot at writing the kind of novel that she likes to read. Her musings and rants can be found on her personal blog, Biel Blather. She is the author of *Good Intentions* (2013), *Hold Her Down* (2014), *I'm Still Here* (2014), *Jump, Jive, and Wail* (2015), *Killing Me Softly* (2015), and *Completions and Connections: A New Beginnings Novella, Book 0* (2015), *Live for This* (2016), and *Made for Me: A New Beginnings Book, Book 1* (2016).

If you've enjoyed this book, please help the author out by leaving a review on Amazon and Goodreads. A few minutes of your time makes a huge difference to an indie author!

www.ingramcontent.com/pod-product-compliance
Lightning Source LLC
Chambersburg PA
CBHW031425020726
47499CB00005B/1605